THE SYN

MY SUNI

DEDICATION

Dedicated to every Beautiful Soul that protects all that is pure while moiling in silence.

THE DEPUTATION

I shouldn't be writing this! Writing isn't my lethal skill and this isn't my Land's encoded language nor the language preceding the '*Super Fissile Vying*'*(SFV)*. Inhabitants like me come from all surviving and far lands and we moil for coins silently. Yet; this isn't about me or my imperfect writing dexterity, I am simply prohibited from narrating this.
I have been missing the thrill in my life. The feeling of living carelessly as a wondering minority not trying to fit in. Writing amateur amorous letters not knowing where to begin. But this isn't about my thrill, knowledge or skill. It's the surreal feeling that these two are giving me. A feeling that makes me want to write with all the vocables we could recover from the smouldered rolls of the fading worldly language. Perhaps for me to remember or to be lost to a destined stranger. Whoever is reading this must correct my imperfect writing in their head and believe they have lived it instead. You can call me '*Papino*' but I am not important. '*Adam*' and '*Orla*' are.

It all started 2 years ago in 2084, 56 years after the SFV that vitiated all super lands and their abettors, when the young suave Adam arrived in a dated metal ship to our sanguine Land '(*F3*)'. Full of hope, Adam wasn't aware of what is awaiting him outside the arrivals port. *Anan* and *Swana*, two mid senior '*oppos*' observing Adam from a distance while pretending to enjoy a beverage across from the port's exit gate. An Oppo or simply an 'O' is a secret term used between us. If only Adam could spot such Os and, more importantly, '*hear them*'.

Anan noticed Swana pulling a small mirror from her red frame bag to fix her flaxen hair and unbutton half of her blue shirt, enough seduction to unintentionally distract him from observing Adam.

Anan. what are you doing?

Swana. Gearing up for duty.

Anan. Button up, Adam is too important to take chances.

Swana. Then why am I here?

Anan. Not sure yet what kind of a gent he is, plus we haven't received instructions from the '*SYN*'.

Swana. Do we even know why we are both here?

Anan. You know we can't ask many questions.

Swana and Anan weren't informed of Adam's importance. His Pre-SFV common name '*Adam*' along with the connotations for his kinfolk (*N1*) and his Land (*S34*) aren't giving any clues of who he could be. The usage of kinfolk and Land connotations has proven crucial in eliminating pre-war judgment and stigma. More importantly, preventing the potential exposure of Pre-SFV affiliations and Land resources.

Adam was admitted into his promised glittering freedom. He stepped out of the port with a smile on his face to ask a stranger for the liveliest road to walk to his new abode. Anan and Swana leave some coins on the table and walk behind him while maintaining a distance.

Adam knocks on the door of his new abode. A middle-aged matron opens and welcomes him in. Anan and Swana observe again from a distance.

Swana. So what now?

Anan. We have a safe-abode across the road, We Wait there.

Swana. I left a great prospect who adores me for this?

Anan. This deputation could be your token to freedom, Something about Adam makes him too important for our '*Patron*'. Be patient.

But Swana is never patient unless she is around a subject she is assigned to. An alluring, flaxen milky skinned damsel such as her is apathetic having won the Various Victorious Seductive Deputations award. She does what the SYN, short for the '*Syndicate*', requires of her and no more. Anan on the other hand has a tranquil gaze through his unneeded clear glasses with a black frame. He also accepted his fate but believes anything given to him as imperative thus he pays heed. A tractability his proud darker skin kinfolk wouldn't have approved or understood.

Their important subject, Adam, was too excited to rest his eyes despite completing a long journey, he wanted to explore the abode's surroundings but the abode owner was too curious to get to know him. Not sure if she is an O of us but doesn't seem the breed. One thing for certain, they all like the chatter.

Anan. Adam seems chatty and he let's out what's in his heart with caution. He seems to be smart but inexperienced. A quality our Patron admires.

Swana. This can't be the reason we are dying here of boredom. He needs endless training to gain on at his age.

Anan. It won't be a struggle, he is still 21. At least you are finally thinking and not only following the Patron's orders blindly since your teenage days.

Swana. I have contributed more to the SYN in the last couple of years than you will ever do in your entire metier.
Anan. Hold it, he is leaving.

Adam steps out of the abode again smiling with excitement to casually saunter around the area. F3, such as the case with other far lands, has lost ingenious means of transportation after the SFV with no remaining unclear energy sources from vanished lands. F3 inhabitants relied on walking or simpler means of tech such as bikes. Adam doesn't mind it having been raised on the toughness of S34 mountains. He made stops at every shop inquiring about everything his eyes saw with an endless lust for knowledge. His curiosity is evident to everyone he meets but never a bothersome. He then sauntered to the high Riddle Bridge crossing the Grand River. It's unknown why its called the Riddle Bridge, many incidents occurred over the bridge so the name fits it's secrets.

Adam eventually became less excited, the area seemed too quiet for his ambitious soul. But he keeps his kind smiley face to everyone he meets nonetheless and appears genuine, easily trusted and always finds a reason to start pleasant conversations with all inhabitants. His ravishing look plays a part; still, Adam must come from a bloodline that influences his indulgent attitude. And this attitude and lack of experience will cost him when dealing with the SYN's hungry Os.

ADAM'S SHIELD

Swana. I wish I could say I missed seeing you on my vacation Anan but I didn't. What have you been up to the last two months?.

Anan. I know the feeling, working without your constant nagging felt like a vacation.

Swana. I know you adore me through these useless black framed glasses, you just keep everything inside as you do with deputations.

Anan. Your confidence supersedes your alluring beauty, I'll give you that. Besides, you know how shallow Os' relationships are so don't even try.

Swana. Seriously what's with those glasses? Has anyone asked you?

Anan. Hard for your undeciphered mind to understand.

Swana. Come on, do tell.

Anan. I use those glasses as a reminder to stay patient

and in character while seeing through inhabitants.

Adam steps out of a lecture hall talking to a damsel and Swana notices.

Swana. Is that Adam?

Anan. Yes... Wait! Where are you going?

Swana. Protecting my token to freedom from that trull.

Anan. Relax she is an O.

Swana. Why the rush? You couldn't wait until I come back? Or am I too dumb to attend a prestigious school?

Anan. Our Patron wanted a damsel his age who fully understands his ancient dogma and literature. We aren't taking risks remember?...

Swana. Are you trying to make it worse?!

Anan. Swana! Alright let's both calm down...Don't get me wrong, I didn't mean you are old or won't figure him out, we just wanted a damsel being herself and not pretending. I have been observing Adam for a couple of months and he is curious and smart; besides, we still don't know much about him or why he is important.

Swana. Why am I here again? A mentor?

Anan. Exactly, the damsel is a natural but a probationer.

Adam leaves the damsel with a smile. A good sign that didn't last long as he seemed indifferent afterwards. He became more of a listener. He started talking less and empathizing more with her stories. He continued to be very kind to her and generous despite his limited coins.

It was a matter of time when the probationer O became less responsive to Swana's demands and more caring towards Adam. She argued it was all part of the plan but it was obvious to Swana that she found refuge in him. She needed to be reminded of the deputation; however, Adam needs not notice a shift in her behavior, a dilemma for Anan who recommended her and Swana whose ticks and mentorship couldn't penetrate Adam's natural defenses. Adam seems to have a genuine power over inhabitants' hearts. He makes them feel cherished, a neural resistance that triumphs over the SYN's venom. Still; the O had to learn the cost of failure.

Anan. Did you ask our O to become godly? Adam isn't that spiritual.

Swana. No, we gave her a visit and she is now rebelling. Adam changed her without ever touching her!

Soon enough things escalated with the young O, Adam noticed her wrist was covered up, at a closer look it appeared to be a wound. He seems hesitant to ask her what happened as the wound seems self-inflicted. Adam insists on carrying the tray of beverages to the O's table after spending his coins. He then couldn't resist asking her. She was prepared to minimize and deflect like they taught her but not for the same reason. She didn't want to disappoint Adam and simply said it was a boiling beverage she accidentally poured on her skin.

Anan. What happened to her? This is not good and Adam doesn't seem to believe her either.

Swana. She couldn't take it anymore with all the guilt.

Some inhabitants aren't meant for what we do especially around someone like Adam.

Anan. So she tried to...

Swana. Yes, and we intervened and saved her. She doesn't know much so she can walk away after this deputation, we agreed.

Adam and the O never saw each other again after their lectures concluded. Adam didn't seem to understand why the O cut all contact. He must have felt she used him for educational assistance. He may never know.

Swana. That's one win for Adam. What now? Can we at least know what the obsession with him is all about?

Anan. You better smarten up, you can't be alluring forever.

Swana. I will always be alluring but can't wait for the day I am no longer needed. I have enough coins for early retirement and I know a far, far away beachy land.

Anan. If you want to be free then leave the thinking to me and remember we can't ask questions... Still, I wish I could say it's not getting personal with Adam.

Swana. I am with you. Let me choose the next O to seduce him. You make sure he has a retinue of Os to steer him toward mine.

Word spread out between the SYN's Os of the lucrative challenge. Adam; however, noticed he is becoming more popular, not just one damsel but multiple of all breads competing for his attention, new friends offering assistance, advice and direction. He didn't mind it at all and took advantage of it all leaving the SYN with a confused group of Os that wonder why they are Adam's retinue. This infuriated the patron as he wanted Adam's deputation to be off-rolls as much as possible and decided to become more involved.

Anan. I will never listen to you again Swana! The Patron now wants a daily rundown, we should have put our pride aside in dealing with Adam.

Swana. I didn't recommend you make a stupid proclamation. Just a few Os around him.

Anan. The Patron also ordered me to let Adam decide what he wants without interference. We will make sure he gets his wishes without influence and see what he is into. Will use any mistake he makes in time. If he doesn't make any, we will entrap him with something.

Swana. Seems like our Patron has plans for Adam, more than curious about him. I hope we aren't stressing out for one potential O!

ADJUSTING LIVES

Adam started looking for independence and earning more coins. He was granted the land's permission to moil. Anan obliquely acted and sent help and guidance his way. Adam took it without hesitation. He didn't seem to notice his good fortune was just an order the SYN has had made.

He soon started the enjoyment of earning coins and learning a new trade. More importantly, helping inhabitants with what he does best, making them feel special and cherished. But something wasn't enumerating. He again noticed that he is being treated abnormally among his hobnobbers as his every move is celebrated, or at least recognized.

Swana. Are we now positioning Adam to become a star without an endgame or at least a leash?

Anan. The patron must have a plan.

Swana. To make him an O? We were disparate and struggling before being chosen by the SYN.

Anan. Ever wonder why? almost all of us.

Swana. Because we were careless and needed the SYN's discipline.

Anan. Yes, that's what they told us.

Swana. What do you mean?

Anan. Nothing, sometimes I wonder if anything that happened to us before being chosen was a coincidence. I mean look at what we are doing now to Adam. We aren't even sure if the SYN existed or had such affairs before the SFV.

Swana. But none of us is Adam. There are many like us, we are dispensable. Let's be grateful for such an honour and all the coins that we can spend quietly until we earn our freedom!

Anan. We are important, don't let your obedience and sweettraps make you think otherwise. As the Patron said, '*if only Os and the SYN existed proceeding the SFV we would have stopped it*'.

Swana. Adam is penetrating your pate! We are both good at this and I am as curious and mostly frustrated but I know my place and my past life always reminds me.

A few more months have passed and Adam's fortune seems to have changed. Every move he makes is now scrutinized more than his hobnobbers without a solid reason. He needed the coins but he kept his pride and he fought, although hesitantly, for his rights.

Anan. I told you the patron has a plan.

Swana. It doesn't seem to be working. He is still

hardheaded. If the SYN needs a disparate Adam, they need to try harder.

Anan. This is just the beginning.

Swana. How long are we stuck with this Adam!? We move on every year, this is becoming more frustrating than personal.

Anan. Miss having a new gent every year?

Swana. I'll do whatever the SYN requires of me until I retire with the gent of my dreams. Plus most of those gents have been easy and boring. I am not even allowed to keep their gifts!

Anan. So what breed of gents are you into?

Swana. So you do care after all.

Anan. Forget it.

Swana. I won't tell. But I won't lie, I have recently been fancying Adam. I hate him but I am lusting for the thrill and victory of winning this debonair gent's heart and then shredding him to pieces for all the SYN's Os to see. It will be a pleasurable spectacle and a worthy permission to my freedom.

Anan. I was informed the Patron has personally chosen a damsel for Adam. Once Adam is desperate enough, she will be revealed.

Swana. Again!! I know more about Adam than all the doxies at the SYN and all the useless Os. Have you ever cared to suggest me?

Anan. I did, the patron said Adam is a curious inhabitant

and is becoming more suspicious. We can't figure him out or his story but we know he is adventurous so she will satisfy that. I don't know who is the chosen one but she is studying him through our rolls and crafting her story accordingly. I also heard she is tantalizing and comely.

Swana. That harlot better not ruin our deputation or I will find her and retire in a slammer instead of a beach!

Little did Swana and Anan know the Patron had more plans for Adam, something that has never been done since, or probably before, the SFV. The Patron is losing a grip on his reputation and started losing patience with Adam. For that he didn't only choose a super O to seduce him but also another O, the only one he truly trusts 'Orla'.

Adam requested time off moiling to have all his four wisdom teeth removed. He was completely out during this supposedly normal procedure as recommended by the surgeon. After a few hours, he woke up with a pate pain and was informed it was a result of a complication from the Anastasia. He passed out gain to only wake up the next day in another room. The surgeon informed Adam that he had more complications from the Anastasia but the operation went well overall and nothing to worry about.

Swana. Looks like this gent's wisdom teeth are as stubborn as him.

Anan. Give Adam a break. He is alone in this land doing it all by himself.

Swana. Since when have you developed a heart? We never feel for our subjects.

Anan. I never said care, just understand his situation. No

wonder you are only good at one thing.

Swana. What the tophet is that supposed to mean?!

Anan. Nothing to worry about as the new supper O will be taking that over and most of our moiling load.

Swana. Was she announced?!

Anan. Yes, no one seems to know her. She is assigned only to important subjects like Adam. The reason why a few of us will ever cross her path.

Swana. She can have him all day. I need time for self-amouring and frolicking!

Adam is still recovering and barely eating, mostly enjoying tomato soup as he learned to make from his progenitress. Bored of his surroundings, he decided to take a short trip to his favourite borough. His usual routine when visiting the borough was to enjoy the nightly mirth and a visit to his favourite library if we can classify it as such, the following afternoon. Only this time it won't be the usual, the Supper O will be waiting for him.

Adam walks into the library full of fiction and twisted antecedents to the SFV, finds an easy read, an empty seat and orders his usual cup of delicacy. He glanced around to see the inhabitants with his graceful smile. He then noticed an alluring damsel wearing a beguiling vermilion dress walking from one-quarter of the library to the one facing him carrying a paperback with a marking inside in one hand and a cup in the other, indicating she had been there for a while just changing seats. As soon as she sets she gazes at Adam with a tantalizing smile on her face.

Adam was enthralled by her voluptuous figure; Still, by now he has learned to resist easily attainable destinations. The alluring Supper O kept on seeking his attention from across the aisle, but he noticed again and again ignored. After a while, he walked away from her view to find a more readable treatise and took his time when he noticed the Super O leaving. He rushed to stop her at the door, he didn't even know the reason. He felt he was about to miss a turn to an adventurous road that wasn't a planned coincident.

Adam introduced himself and pretended not to know his way around the borough and she hesitantly agreed to be his guide. He asked for her name and simply said 'Sigi' They had a delightful chatter until he took his chance to ask her out.

Adam. So tell me Sigi, where will I find you?

Sigi. I can be where you tend to like.

Adam. Promise you will be there?

Sigi. I promise.

Adam has told Sigi where the rendezvous will be and went to his abode feeling uneasy yet excited about the prospect. Sigi is comely, brown-eyed brunette and too flawless to be non-fictional. He wondered if she was of his creed and wisdom, little did he know her best skill other than being alluring is being astute. He wouldn't have noticed this, as for the first time, he had no control but to wait for an adventurous road only to have slipped into a long dark tunnel leading to Sigi's hidden ship.

Anan. And she did it!

Swana. I would have done it better.

Anan. I thought you would have appreciated your kind of talent.

Swana. I wouldn't have worn a blazing red dress in a library that screams, dear inhabitants, look at me!

Anan. Affirmative, you use more skin and less fabric for that right?

Swana. Oh Anan, it's pointless to educate a gent like you that wouldn't notice the difference.

Anan. Withal, she fixed it by leaving, which made him feel it was a coincidence.

Swana. Now what?

Anan. We wait for any assistance she may require. She can't be alone.

The next day Adam went to the agreed corner of the borough park and waited for Sigi. She was late but she came over prepared wearing a Roseate dress. Not what Adam seems to appreciate, an effortless enchantress is what seems to stupefy him. They had late edibles, listened to a live recital and she opened up about her woes. Adam gave her words of wisdom and wanted her to feel special and cherished as he always does. He insisted on walking her to her abode and she hesitantly accepted. He felt she was not all-wise but smart and special.

Adam. Can I see you tomorrow?

Sigi. I have a lecture to attend. How about the day after?

Adam. That will be delightful.

On the third day, Adam took Sigi to the beach and had a feeling she wasn't being herself. Something is anomalous but for the first time, he didn't want to know what it was. He encouraged her to not over-prepare and to be herself, the ravishing damsel she is.

Walking down the beautiful roads of the borough, a few inhabitants passing by offered compliments to both of them, one matron said to Adam 'What a ravishing Damsel you have, don't lose her' an affirmation Adam delighted by and wasn't expecting. He will never realize the matron was also an O of us to subtly influence him in his decision to keep Sigi.

Adam spent the night at Sigi's abode since he didn't expect to reserve one in the borough but he never made any naughty dalliance. His intention was to carefully know a damsel he could eventually wed, instead, he must have sensed Sigi was steering her sail towards his wind, and she was ready for all subsequent moves. He felt she had done this before and was either worried about losing him or him uncovering her truth. Adam travelled back to his abode and started having headaches. Sigi's covert ship was about to rotate upside down and Adam will fall from it into the sea of verities and theatrics thus twisting the essence of what it means to be free.

ORLA

Orla. Hi Adam

Adam. Great! What is happening to my pate now?. More rest it is for such a hallucination.

Orla. You are not hallucinating Adam. I can explain why you can hear me in your pate, I just want you to kindly listen.

Adam. What is this, am I thinking and talking to myself without opening my lips? this doesn't sound like me. Oh Sigi, you must have left something in my cup.

Orla. She didn't do this to you, now please listen. I can explain, just focus on what I have to say.

Adam. What is this? go on my head, stupefy me.

Orla. I didn't expect this would work but it did so let me first say my name is Orla. Secondly, I apologize because this is all my fault.

Adam. Can you get out of my pate or tell me what is happening already?

Orla. I never thought of the day I would talk to you, yet, there is so much to say and I didn't plan it this fast. Please take your time to digest it all. Promise you won't act recklessly and I promise that I will fix all of this.

Adam. Just go on, will you!

Orla. You had a wisdom teeth removal. Remember the complications?

Adam. Yes, what about it?

Orla. We inserted a contraption into your brain through your sinuses during that surgery.

Adam. What contraption?!! Who is we? How can you read my thoughts!!

Orla. I can't read your thoughts, that was the original plan which failed. Just please let me explain one point at a time. It will take a while and I hope you understand that I am here to help you.

Adam. Let me lay down first, such pain .... go on I am listening.

Orla. Again my name is Orla and I am a neurology tutee. More momentously, I moil for SYN. I will explain later what we do but for now, you need to understand that the contraption inserted in your pate was supposed to be completely removed as it failed during the surgery but it had three components. One was attached to read your thoughts which was the main goal and it failed and another to analyze your intention to communicate and was unwittingly detached and remained inside your pate. The third to mirror all your senses but was risky to remove so it remained as well.

Adam. What!? Why would anyone want to read my thoughts and analyze my feelings?

Orla. Adam please, I promise to explain everything in time.

Adam. I need to go for a walk and clear my thoughts, maybe it will clear you too.... No offense, I need to walk.

Orla. Please don't, at least not now. There are two oppos outside your abode and will watch your every move once you step out. They will eventually sense something is wrong with you.

Adam. Am I in danger?

Orla. No, I am the only one who knows about this but if someone finds out I will be, then you.

Adam. Why are you telling me this? Why should I even trust you?

Orla. You don't have to, but time will prove everything I say to be the truth. Especially now that you met Sigi.

Adam. How do you know about Sigi? What does she have to do with this?

Orla. She is not who she pretends to be, I read your rolls so I know you are smart enough to notice. I rushed to contact you to warn you about her.

Adam. She has done nothing wrong and asked for nothing.

Orla. For now, she will eventually have something on you or will entrap you if needed. That's why I instanter decided to warn you when I felt the signal from the senses contraption. What I am about to say should get me expatriated for years. So don't make me regret this. I know you have a wandering mind and will have endless questions but you have always been wise and patient. Please be patient now and understand the severity of my situation.

Adam. I am listening Orla but don't do or say anything for me that will get you punished, I am not asking for any of this.

Orla. I am doing it to clear my conscious. I know you are a smart benevolent gent and will eventually understand.

Adam. continue ...

Orla. Sigi moils for the SYN as well, she is a Supper O reserved for high-value subjects.

Adam. What is an O? And Sin as in sinful?

Orla. I guess that fits what we do but no it's actually S.Y.N. Informal code for the Syndicate. And O is a secretive term we use among each other referring to us, oppos.

Adam is always thrilled to discover life for his own fascination. He has more courage than fear but is always cautious to enter an everlasting trap or hurt others along his adventurous road. Had he fully understood what Orla just did, he would have stopped her for her own sake. By delating Sigi, Orla just crossed a gate from darkness into an inflamed road that she can't cross back through to her semi-normal life. She might be one of the smartest, but if the SYN finds out, she will be expatriated and her life will never be restless after this sacrilege. There must be more to Orla's valour than mere feelings for Adam or clearing her conscious. Os know the consequences of delating the SYN and other Os.

The SYN subsists clinching enigmatic prerogative powers. It's all grounded on the fear of the failure to prevent the SFV by whatever murky powers that could have preceded it. Antecedents to the SFV are not immutable. The SYN is shaped by mastery donated by the *'Family'* and the assistance of the *'Subterranean Oligarchs'*. They were the only inhabitants to shield knowledge and coins when the Superlands of west and east collided and all vanished. Ostensibly, SFV fomented over the holiest of lands, and a saviour who never manifested. The preponderance of inhabitants perished and those who survived forsaken ancient dogmas. This all ensued in a single generation. We in the far lands, along with a few surviving lands, are the remaining credence, each hiding its riches and salvaged weaponry. The SYN, with the undeclared influence of the Family, is mutely swaying unaware inhabitants to the unknown superbness. Orla couldn't have known or allowed to know this and question the rectitude of the SYN. She must have another spur to delating Os to Adam.

Adam. Will this pate pain ever vanish?

Orla. Soon enough. I had the same amount of pain after my operation which was a few days before yours but I slept more hours than I could ever remember in my life after receiving your signal which was unexpected. I rushed to have another operation with a contraption that can send signals so I can communicate with you.

Adam. Why are you endangering yourself?

Orla. Os call me the decent one. But even I have done enough to divert inhabitants' paths toward the SYN without knowing why. A few times I became aware late.

Adam. Has the SYN always been this evil? What's their truth?

Orla. Many Os including me have lost sight of the good the SYN has done to our land and probably others, now that I have come to think about it. We were always reminded of the honour it was to moil for the land but what we now see in the day is always overshadowed by what we did at night at the SYN's orders. The more nights I moiled for them, the less I could close my eyes and never want to wake up.

Adam. I might not understand all of this but I sense that you are cleansing your soul, and I commend you for this. I still want to understand what all this has to do with me.

Orla. The SYN is not aware of my deputation with you. Only the Patron and even he thought the contraption failed so I was no longer needed. I trusted what he wanted me to do was to make the SYN virtuous again and save future Os from daily misery.

Adam. Orla, although your senses aren't mirrored to me, I sense your sadness but I also want to make sense of what you are telling me. Share up, and kindly be clear.

Orla. Apologies Adam, we always whisper when we chat to each other about our affairs with the SYN. I will try my best to explain.

Orla opened up all closed doors to Adam. At least all the doors opened to her. The more she elucidated her world, the more Adam realized his new beloved land was becoming more of a fancy dining hall on a ship with no guests allowed into the grimy galley. Those invited to the galley will never savour the ships' edibles again. The only way out is by jumping off the ship and swimming unswervingly into an uncertain destiny.

Nevertheless, Adam has always been sanguine and, more importantly sensible. He soon realized the importance of the SYN, the ship needs a galley, the grim galley needs not be grim, a constant purification and a way to truly ensure it is what was needed.

Adam. Are there good Os to advance only the good deeds of the SYN?

Orla. There used to be. No one now dares to wonder or even whisper, let alone oppose or even worse '*expose*'.

Adam. Sounds like a torture for pure souls. Again what part am I playing in all of this? I have always taken the straight path and would never join anything that resembles the SYN.

Orla. That's what I and many Os have been wondering. You have become famed for the SYN's interest in you and your admirable character.

Adam. Not for my looks?

Orla. That too, but don't get excited. Your looks could be the reason for your downfall. The SYN chooses attractive Os to allure future ones.

Adam. Now be honest Orla, Why me?

Orla. I honestly don't know.

Adam. I don't mean the SYN, I meant you. Why did you decide to help me?

Orla. I have come to realize that you are a benevolent gent. That was enough to protect you; still, when I was given this deputation it was not to be written in the SYN's rolls or yours. This is a serious breach that I thought the Patron wanted to use for the goodness of the SYN and Land.

Adam. What goodness would that be? Especially since I will again never join the SYN.

Orla. Many have said that before you Adam. The SYN always finds a way. I trusted the Patron, and truly believed in the goodness of the SYN and what must be done so I felt he chose you to cleanse it in time. You are adventurous, kind, and trustworthy. But the best quality of all is incorruptible.

Adam. And I thought it was my charm.

Orla. This is serious Adam!

Adam. Fine, what changed?

Orla. I now believe the Patron chose you for the '*Blau Family*', not the SYN or the land, that's why they sent Sigi who is a member of the Family.

Adam. Great! More unwanted guests in my party. Who's the Blau Family? and why would they be interested in me?

Orla is getting too attached to Adam. The Os go to extreme length to earn the trust of their subjects. Giving them personal, life and even some SYN's tricks to earn such a valuable trust. Nonetheless, none is allowed or even dares to mention the Blau Family.

The SYN has continuously used by the Family but it was obvious the SYN was becoming the Family's chaperone. Orla is too young to even know much about the Blau Family. The last time there was a discussion about the Family's influence within the SYN's hidden boundaries was over a decade ago when the '*Laman Hamlet*s' affair got out of the SYN's control.

THE LAMAN HAMLET

The Laman Hamlet was a beautiful peaceful hamlet that one of our veteran Os retired in. It had a basic livelihood, no major markets or means for entertainment and most of the abodes were dated. The people enjoyed the basics, the charming scenery, farming and fishing from the river which was their main source of living besides trading their woodwork and knotted pile carpets. The classic basic peaceful living that the older half of our retired Os seek to forget their past.

The story goes that over a decade ago the Family was looking to develop a new land while using its inhabitants as laborers with their never-ending pill of coins. They used their own Os within the SYN to find such a land, to screen its inhabitants and any potential resistance. One O was taking a long adventurous road trip when he lost his way to arrive at the Laman Hamlet, he was graciously hosted and fed by the chief's 20-years-old son, the O's age.

The O couldn't believe his good fortune and found an excuse to stay longer with the inhabitants of the hamlet. He quickly realized the youths of the hamlet were snuffy by the lack of modern life, a frustration that worries the Chief as the migration of youths was on the rise.

The O left the Hamlet to debrief the SYN before the Family chooses another land. The Family was quite gruntled with the O's briefing and rewarded him with an elevating opportunity, to become the main O of the deputation. He is to contact the chief's younger son as the owner's nephew of a developing Firm. He is to convince the him that he appreciated their generosity and that he fell in Amour with the inhabitants and wanted to help them have a modern life. The Chief's older son was suspicious of the firm's motives in such a remote Hamlet. But the Chief always admired the younger son's ambition. Besides, he couldn't risk the migration of more youth thus he gave the 'Blue Firm' his blessings. The SYN sent enough Os for every scenario that might unfold. The Family doesn't take chances when it comes to dispensing their coins.

The Blue Firm began with developing the 'Blue Tower' that offered habitation to half of the hamlet's inhabitants, a dining hall and a nightly entertainment act for the youth to rejoice.

Soon enough a few of the younger wedded inhabitants traded their abodes in the Hamlet to the Blue Firm to have the pleasure of living in the Blue Tower. The youth started rejoicing more and moiling less thus farmlands were turning pale. Those of wedding age elected a hidden lucrative life with the seductive newcomers, a few of whom were Os of the Family.

The Chief quickly developed an unidentified illness that the Hamlet's healers couldn't cure. The main O noticed a sadness in the chief's only daughter. He pressed her to know what was keeping her sorrowful. She trusted him after all that he had done for their hamlet and his relationship with her brother and told him of her poppa's illness, he promised her that he would do all he could to help him and requested healers from the mainland. The Chief's health stabilized but wasn't cured and needed constant treatment.

The Chief's older son knew the wind was changing too fast for Laman. Not only pulling off its trees but also their roots. He begged his poppa to act. But nothing could the ageing Chief do. The inhabitants are now seduced, have their own dreams and entanglements and won't visit his wisdom like before. Even if they revisit such wisdom, the Chief's blessings to the Blue Firm obliged him to remain with it without enough coins to satisfy its departure.

The eldest son decided to act, he roamed around the main lands and triumphantly persuaded a developing firm, the '*collectif Firm*', using the success of the Blue Firm. The Chief blessed this news and competition for Laman's sake. The collectif Firm was not perfect but less demanding and less interested in their way of life.

Needless to say, The Family heard of the new Firm from the many Os they have installed in the Hamlet. They have naturally suppressed such competition in other lands and this was no different.

The main O, who the chief's son had welcomed, had started an indecent affair with the Chief's daughter, the fetching young damsel celebrated by the village who fell for him after he treated her poppa. Little did she know that he made sure this affair can be publicized when needed, the affair is punishable under the village's centuries-old traditions. The chief won't be able to save his daughter and himself from such a disgrace and punishment.

An epistle arrived from the Blue Tower's main floor to the chief's older son. 'let's have a chatter'. The Chief's older son was excited about the prospect hoping the blue Firm would make concessions and bow to the competition and make things right thus he went to the rendezvous.

He was offered to abandon the idea of the new Firm and competition in exchange for a new massive abode for himself with half the cost payable over 20 years. He was also offered a symbolic managerial role in the Blue Tower with valuable coins to pay for the abode and more. All this to make sure he stays on a leash.

The chief's son furiously stood up and said. *'I might not know what your nirvana is, and we might be simpler inhabitants but we have wisdom that the centuries carved in us that won't be scrubbed off by your coins'.*

The Firm's head also an O replied 'We understand that you are the wisest in Laman that's why we offered you the role. Take your time to think about it and all that we can do together. One last thing, this travelling bag came to us anonymously. We always help needy people in the village but this was anything but ordinary and it was meant for your poppa the Chief. However; we believe you should have it since he is not well and it only makes sense that you take care of such unfortunate events. Again we are counting on your wisdom to work with us'.

The older son left the tower with the travelling bag and opened it as soon as he was alone in his abode. In it something revealing of his sister's affair with the Firm's main O. He knew the Blue Firm was impacting inhabitants' abodes, little did he know it was inside them.

The poor older son had big dreams for his Hamlet yet his sister and poppa were more important. Even though the Blue Firm never threatened him, it was obvious he needed to comply.

The older son asked his poppa to abandon the new Firm as a misjudgment on his part and to continue with the inhabitants inside the Blue Tower until he finds another firm. The Chief noticed that his son's excitement has vanished and his mood changed from anger to sadness and no more words of wisdom.

The older son rejected the abode and post-offer but gave the Blue Firm what they wanted, an enclosed playfield for their unknown nirvana and the Collectif Firm left the village with his dreams.

The retired O living in Laman was carefully watching his beloved retirement Hamlet becoming a puppets' land. He knew enough of the Family's ways and broke into the older son's abode to find the traveling bag and discover the daughter's affair. He respected the Chief but knew what needed to be done. Soon enough, the whole Hamlet found out all the Family's malicious conduct and that the sickness of the Chief was the Blue Firm's doing as well since he constantly enjoyed the edibles at the Blue Tower. All Os were taken hostages by the hamlet's enraged inhabitants. The Chief's daughter couldn't see her poppa's shame and used his ancient blade on the main O to clear the Chief's shame and her pate marking him gone in the river, she wanted to be gone too but the retired O intervened. The inhabitants released the tower's Os for releasing the chief and Laman from their blessings to the Blue Firm without any coins.

The Family and SYN knew the exposure was the marking of an experienced O. The retired O was found then never found. It was a lesson for all Os and the last time an insider ever dared to expose the Family.

Orla. That was the last story I could find in the SYN's hidden rolls and elders' chatter about the Family.

Adam. So the Family does some good. They help some lands flourish but their ways are dark and they unfairly suppress competition. Are there decent members within the family?

Orla. There are. In fact, The Blau Family are decedents of a great linage full of morals and contribution to most lands but as with all kinfolks, a time comes when new heirs are driven by greed and lust for control, they found enough inhabitants willing to do anything for coins after the SFV and kept enough eyes in every SYN to feed them with everyone's rolls.

Adam. Is the Family ever subsiding? Surely they can't continue without opposition.

Orla. Coins Adam, Coins.

Indeed coins, but also fear. Orla seems to know more than she could reveal. She must have read rolls prerogative of the elders. What Adam has to do with it all is higher than any O could decipher. Was it all an unplanned coincidence? The elder's deputation? The Family's? Or is it just Adam's providence? Time and Os will tell.

THE THEATRICS

Swana. I didn't beat all the doxies to wait days in this room for his majesty to make a move.

Anan. At least you are thinking. Adam hasn't left his abode in two days.

Swana. We need eyes and ears in there. Where is the Super O?

Anan. She isn't part of our deputation, we can't ask. Adam will eventually need edibles.

Orla. Adam.

Adam. Yes.

Orla. Sorry to wake you up. The Os outside must be noticing a change in your behavior. You need to go out as usual and contact Sigi too, she moved to your area.

Adam. So I need to pretend that I care like an O? that nothing is happening?

Orla. It will be easy for you. You are a natural.

Adam. I guess I can but not with Sigi. I want to be with someone I can wed. Not to forget, I can be nice to inhabitants, empathize and help with their trauma but I can't be myself with a damsel who's pretending with me and can never be my vrou.

Orla. You have to Adam. She needs not observe any change in your behaviour for your sake and mine. Plus the Family will keep sending you more Sigis, might as well be her.

Adam. I have always lived a genuine life without fear. But I will do this for your safety.

Orla. Thanks Adam. I will do my all to protect you too.

Anan. He is moving. Let's move!

Swana. Finally! I need to walk and see some pretty faces. Tired of yours.

Anan. At least you find my face pretty.

Swana. Not the prettiest but at least I am not pretending with you. I just feel comfortable around you.

Anan. What are you doing..Stop it!... last time unbuttoned your shirt for Adam, now trying to unbutton mine. Just remember I am not Adam, I have tutored Os your bread. It won't work on me.

Swana. Enough with the disciplined theatrics. This deputation will apparently take forever. We only have each other if you know what I mean.

Anan. Not a chance, just focus on Adam for your retirement sake.

Adam walks to Sigi's abode and throws a stone at her window. Seems like a pre-SFV romantic gesture. She opens the window and sees Adam waiting for her with a smile on his face and an Adrenalin Rose in his hand that he picket along the way. Adam just assuaged her fears of failing. Still; she needs to to keep the theatrics.

Sigi. What do you want Adam?

Adam. This Rose needs a vase I thought you would have the best one.

Sigi. Even if I do, a caring gent needs to pass by and water it nightly.

Adam. I adore this Rose so I'll eagerly pass by.

Sigi. Promise?

Adam. I promise.

Sigi. Alright, I am coming. Give me time.

Adam. Time is the least I can give you.

Sigi keeps Adam waiting although she was primed for his visit having access to Anan's fresh rolls. She opens for him, takes the Rose and he gives her a gentle kiss on the cheek. While she stayed in character.

Adam. I could get used to this scent.

Sigi. I can sell you the bottle.

Adam. Nothing for free in this Land.

Sigi. I am just a tutee.

Adam. Must come with your soft skin then.

Sigi. That comes with a soul that you can't afford.

Even though it's all theatrics, Os almost never mention the soul in their deputations. Their encephalons have lost it's connotation and their tongues can't bear it's weight. Sigi must be an anomalous supper oppo to remember it, or a piece of her soul hasn't been pilfered by the Family.

Adam. What am I doing here Orla?

Orla. Being a gent in a relationship.

Adam. Pretending to be for once in my life.

Orla. It is still you in there. Just be yourself.

Adam. Can you see what I am seeing?

Orla. Yes, all your senses are shared with me.

Adam. Where is Sigi?

Orla. You are looking at her cooking in the open kitchen, wearing a pleated green skirt. She learned your taste in modest minimalistic beauty.... Lucky you.

Adam. Lucky? I am not interested in her anymore.

Orla. I meant the edibles, I am famished. You get to eat and I only get to taste.

Adam. Can you turn it off from your end?

Orla. I can't, I kept the permanent contraption after my surgery for future experiments. That's what I at least told the surgeon and patron. They don't know I later added the sending component so I can communicate with you.

Adam. Speaking of taste. I have a tasteless question.

Orla. I might not be able to read your thoughts but I know you enough. Things will happen between you too. Just ignore I am here.

Adam. How could I?

Orla. We were edified by the SYN from emotions. Affections have no meanings to us while in deputations. And we have watched many others at it too.

It is true that over the years, Os loose their affections from all the theatrics. Nothing left in them but a transient thrill. Orla; however, wasn't honest with Adam. She hasn't been in such intimate deputations. The Patron always favoured her bright mind over her beauteous body for the advancement of the SYN's goals. She still has a soul and affection that she could lose if Adam loses his.

Sigi. I am not the best cook but I made this for you.

Adam. I adore edibles yet overly famished to judge this one. so you get an unconscious endorsement.

Sigi. Then I better start learning quickly.

Adam. It is actually delicious.

Sigi. You sound surprised. I am not that bad of a cook.

Adam. I wouldn't know the difference when looking at those eyes.

Sigi. Your tongue must have said this to many eyes before.

Adam. Yet, I am here looking at yours. Now come closer.

Swana. He is going for it!... You better not close that curtain Sigi and stay in the damn entertainment zone.

Anan. She knows we are watching so don't hope for a show. Here she goes, closing the curtains.

Swana. That Trull! Why can't we have orbs in there!? We are the same troupe!

Anan. No we are not. She is of a different guild. Plus calm down, you are always raunchy.

Swana. It's the only thrill I have besides coins. That is until I am decommissioned. Unlike you always frigid!

Anan. Just with you. I just have a better taste in damsels.

Swana. No O has figured your taste, always lonely on deputation. Still; Kind of desirable I have to admit.

Anan. How many times have I said it won't happen?

Swana. Fine. Let me just fantasize about those too in peace.

Orla on the other hand isn't conceptualizing, she sees what Adam sees and even recognized Orla's scent. She can feel Orla's soft skin as if she was between both of them. But Orla had only one matter occupying her Pate. A matter the failed contraption would have answered. Adam's thoughts. Is Adam beguiled by Sigi? The SYN would long for a positive confirmation, not Orla.

Adam. Good morning Orla.

Orla. Good morning Adam. How was your night?

Adam. You have seen it all so no point in remembering.

Orla. I was dozed actually. Still; I hope you had a pleasant time... By the way, was she as good as we heard?

Adam. It was all theatrics from both of us. Besides, I feel uneasy discussing this.

Orla. Apologies, we are used to this kind of discussions at the SYN. There is no such thing as subjects' privacy. Plus I haven't talked to outsiders for a while.

Adam. You had edibles? You were famished last night.

Orla. No I was too tired and dozed quickly.

Adam. What was the last scene you remember?

Orla. When you were complimenting her eyes.

Adam. Let me bring you some edibles. I can leave it near your abode.

Orla. Thanks Adam, I am fine and will take a walk for it. One unfortunate thing to remember is that you will never see me.

Adam. You don't trust me? I will never expose you.

Orla. I trust you wouldn't. It's not that Adam, we can't be seen together or in the same area as Os will report a suspicious coincidence. That will be the end of this and us.

Adam. How is it fair that I can never see you? I have always lived a freegent.

Orla. We Os are never free. Even subjects such as you mistakenly believe in such a fantasy. The SYN can steer your fate Adam. It's unfair but so many unaware paramours never made it as their amour contradicts the SYN'S plans.

Adam. I would vie endlessly for a damsel I amour.

Orla. I know you would. That's why the SYN hates proud inhabitants like you. You make it harder for them so they make an example of you.

Adam. I only mentioned edibles, how are we now talking about amour?

Orla. I was just making a point Adam. Focus on Sigi and keep her close.

Adam. Can't get closer than this.

Orla. I don't mean her head on your shoulder. I can see that. I mean keep an eye on all her tricks. I will observe and help but even I don't know her kind of entrapments.

It was a cold night for Orla despite feeling the warmth of Adam's body against Sigi's. She couldn't even drowse that night. She is young and beauteous to be lorn. It's partly her choice. Still; she understands the patron will disrupt any plans by gents trying to enter her life. He finds her too precious to be swept away from his own plans.

THE ORBS

Anan. We now have eyes in Adam's abode.

Swana. Are you serious!?

Anan. Got the approbation last night when Adam was away. You were asleep.

Swana. The full fascicle?

Anan. The full fascicle.

Swana. Finally some amusement!

The SYN's approbation means most Os can share Swana's merriment. Adam will commence to attract more admirers within the SYN, tutees will be elevated by such a show and the normalization of subjects' intimacy.

Adam softly leaves bed. Prepares edibles for Sigi and leaves it on a table with a beholden note. Sigi continued with her feigned sleep until his departure. She had enough chatter and fortuity for her rolls and needed no more. She also lets him depart without a sayonara so he lusts for more. Alas for Sigi, Adam is presenting her with the ordinary gentleman and she isn't occupying his mind. He is thinking of the one feeling his skin yet can't feel hers. On the way to his abode, Orla warns him of the SYN's orbs in his abode.

Orla. I need to tell you something Adam.

Adam. The note I left her meant nothing.

Orla. Nothing to do with Sigi... Actually, it might.

Adam. Are you alright? Tell me.

Orla. I am... It's just ...I think your abode might now have orbs.

Adam. Please tell me I am not being watched in my abode.

Orla. I am not sure, I saw some movement in your area. I am sorry Adam but I can't be sure. I haven't been reading your fresh rolls not to raise suspicion. I still don't think they would do it since they need a vindication for such an escalation.

Adam. How can we confirm?

Orla. Just don't think about it. Be yourself, you have never done anything wrong so nothing to worry about.

Adam. I am getting tired of this!

Orla. Be patient. They can't do this forever. They have nothing on you and you are too stubborn to join the SYN or the Family. Add to that, the SYN doesn't have unbounded resources and will eventually give up.

Sanguine Os such as Orla trust in their access to rolls and the 'Unyielding Syndicate Stratagem'(USS). This sanguine view is the disparity between them and the Family's Os. The patron will twist the USS for the Family's aim. More than not, the SYN's arrows will cross the land's sky yet the aim wasn't for it. Sanguine Os will see the arrows in the sky but will never know where they are landing.

Adam finished moiling for coins that day and walked in silence to his adobe. He must have been wondering if this is his destiny, how long will this last, what is the SYN's aim, is he being watched at his abode, and what will Sigi do to him. These thoughts aren't revealed to Orla but she is aware that suspicious subjects have a wandering mind when touched by Os.

Orla. Adam don't forget to water Sigi's rose tonight.

Adam. Do I get a break from pretending

Orla. You promised her. She needs to believe that you are thrilled.

Adam. Nothing exciting about fake kisses.

Orla. Adam... for me.

Adam. Fine for you.

Orla. Before I forget, you have a travelling bag in the emporium across your abode.

Adam. Not expecting any. Form Sigi?

Orla. From me. It's Sigi's birthing carousal. You need to dress well for her tonight.

Adam. I appreciate it but I can't take it. I will get my own.

Orla. Adam. I understand but this is an important theatrics. Plus I know you support your kinfolk.

Adam. That isn't your affair Orla.

Orla. I meant well.

Adam. Regardless ... I simply can't accept it.

Orla. It can't be left there without collection. It will be overly suspicious of your behavior. And I can't do it. I sent an acquisition under your name. Apologies Adam, it won't happen again. Kindly collect it for our sake and the decision of its fate is yours to make.

Adam. I appreciate all that you do for me. I just can't be pretending with you too. Kindly Keep my private affairs and kinfolk out of this.

Orla. Noted. Again, I meant well when I mentioned your kinfolk. Just to be aware, many Os in the SYN including me are aware and admire that your coins are ceded for your kinfolk.

Adam. Thanks for the recognition but I will not indulge in this. I will just collect the traveling bag and contact Sigi.

Proud subjects such as Adam aren't driven by coins, gifts or lust but by a balance of life's pleasures underneath their kinfolk and ancient dogma. A quality the SYN admires and despises simultaneously. As those subjects are trustworthy for the Land but a risk for their villainy.

Adam was short of time and coins so he picked Orla's gift and wore it instead in Sigi's abode. Looking at himself in the mirror with a subtle smile on his face but must have a guilty feeling about being ill-mannered with Orla. His attire fits his body perfectly, he must have remembered his shining days with his kinfolk.

Adam. Orla, What do you think?

Orla. Flawless... She is behind you, looking at you. Don't keep her waiting.

Adam. I would rather not turn around and stay with you.

Orla. Don't be risible Adam. Not now. She is looking!

Adam. Let her wait.

Sigi. When is the grand reveal Mr. Adam

Orla. Adam now!

Adam. What do you think Sigi?

Sigi. I am now wondering whose birthing carousal it is.

Adam. Mine to be celebrated nightly for seeing such eyes.

Sigi. You're good Mr.

Adam. I will not waste your taste in attire.

Sigi. Mine? You must be daydreaming.

Adam. What? Oh am not, I was just thinking about the attire.

Sigi. What about it that is more arresting than my eyes?

Adam. Nothing... actually, your lips are trying hard.

Sigi. Come on Adam what is it? You can open your mind to me.

Adam. This attire was the last one in the emporium and an adorable damsel was holding it and about to buy it, she instead gave it to me. Said it would look better on me.

Sigi. Are you making me jealous? Don't because it is working.

Adam. Not at all. I was just thinking how such a damsel can make a sacrifice for a stranger she might never meet.. I mean meet again.

Sigi. Oh Adam, any damsel would do such a gesture for such a captivating gent. Now let's leave we are late.

After having edibles, Sigi pretended to have lost the keys to her abode. It was her intention to spend the night at his. Adam being the gentleman had no choice but to invite her in for the night. After all it's her birthing carousal.

Adam. Orla are you there? Sorry, I must do this again.

Orla. Nothing to apologize for, it's all a web of deceit.

Sigi. Let me take this attire off you and your pate.

Nothing will take Orla's gift off Adam's mind or him of hers. Orla's mind is too utterly vexed with a damsel taking her gift off Adam's body, the gent she is safeguarding. Through another agonizing night for Orla, she noticed something abnormal and had to warn Adam.

Orla. Adam.

Adam. Not the right time Orla.

Orla. Right.

Adam. Apologies for squelching you earlier. I just couldn't have you in my pate while being too close to her. I meant I want to but she would notice.

Orla. Don't apologize. I thought it might be nothing. It would have been too late to warn you anyway. Plus you would have no choice but to continue with this cruel stagecraft.

Adam. Whatever it is, we will fix it together.

Orla. I don't think we can and won't make a difference now.

Adam. Tell me, what is it?

Orla. I think I have to. Did you notice Sigi periodically concealing her private....?

Adam. I am discomfited talking about this Orla. I thought you would disdain our nightly affair.

Orla. I am but this could be important.

Adam. I did notice. She must be shy.

Orla. We are past that stage of theatrics. It is something else. Your abode must now have orbs.

Adam. I was hoping it was just a suspicion, you think we were watched last night?

Orla. I am afraid it's the most logical reason. Although abnormal for a super O to react to it.

Adam. Is there anything we can do? I can confront her.

Orla. It's too late Adam. The SYN must have received the rolls by now. I haven't been reading your fresh rolls, again to not raise any suspicion. I didn't think they would do it since they again needed a vindication. I failed you Adam, I failed you.

Adam. You didn't. You are doing your best and opening my eyes and I can't ask for more. Was this bound to happen? The orbs?

Orla. Not ultimately but it does happen. I am wondering how could they have approbation for this. Have you said or done anything recently to provoke such an escalation by the SYN? They need vindication for such an advancement.

Adam. Not that I am aware of. I hold forth but nothing in my pate to be of interest to the SYN .. you know that by now.

Orla. Then they besmirched you Adam. You must be frustrating the Patron with your morality, that by itself can be a threat.

Adam. I am not godly Orla. How could I, by simply living, become a threat to someone I never met?

Orla. You give everyone you meet hope. You make them feel special and adored. That's enough hope and courage for Os to resist their fate.

Adam. What are we to do now?

Orla. As long as you aren't to give in, there is nothing to do but continue with the theatrics. The SYN will give up on you eventually but I can't say the same of the Family not knowing their aim.

Adam. It's my fault I brought her here. Actually... Let them have it. I still have no fears. I am still a freegent. This would have happened eventually. Better with a damsel I have no feelings for.

Orla. Just don't let it get to you Adam that's what they want. Be yourself and Live your life. You have never done anything wrong so nothing to worry about.

Adam. I appreciate all that you do for me. I am just getting tired of this.

Orla. Be patient Adam. They can't do this forever. Again, they won't find anything against you unless they try to entrap you. That's why am here to prevent that from ever happening. I am also confident that you are too stubborn to join the SYN or the Family. Aside from orbs, the SYN doesn't have unbounded fresh resources just for you.

Orbs as USS are vital for justice in the Land, howbeit, the preponderance of their findings are harnessed for coercion. It would have been a more favorable outcome for the SYN had Adam been wedded or a famed godly gent. Woefully for them, Adam is neither.

Orla. Looks like she is waking up.

Adam. She is indeed.

Orla. Alright, I will let you two have edibles. Need to make mine. Later Adam.

Adam. I would rather not do anything for her.

Orla. She is a member of the Family but she might still have a heart. Besides, it's Amourday so don't be cruel.

Adam. Right, I forgot. That's enough sign, isn't it?

Orla. I am gone, have fun.

Adam. Wait before you go!.. I want to bring you something for Amourday?

Orla. I forgot I can't be gone. Neither can you. But thanks. Amour isn't a juncture, it's a sempiternal certitude.

Adam. Such beauteous wisdom...She is up, alright later.

Sigi. Good morning Adam.

Adam. Good morning. You were asleep for a while.

Sigi. Apologies Adam but I am not feeling well.

Adam. What are you feeling?

Sigi. Middle and pate pain.

Adam. I'll take you to the infirmary.

Sigi. No, it's not that serious. Just need to rest if my stay in your abode is not bothersome.

Adam. Not at all. You can stay and I won't moil for coins then.

Sigi. You should go, I can't be the reason to lose coins. I will go to my abode instead.

Adam. No stay here and I will go for a short while.

His Kind heart always prevails. Adam quickly forgot Sigi's deputation and only sees a vulnerable damsel and it might not always be theatrics. As soon as Adam leaves, Sigi begins searching his abode after carefully marking where everything was. She doesn't seem to find anything of interest, Someone seems to contact Sigi as she is communicating back. It's not the SYN and she seems to give an angry reply.

Swana. This useless doxie better find something there. Even her performance with Adam was sluggish last night. He must have been bored of her.

Anan. She is good, look at her searching everywhere.

Swana. Are we planting seeds in there?

Anan. The patron wouldn't want to frame Adam this quickly not knowing his reaction. He has a fighting spirit and coercion might boomerang. An ostracized Adam is useless to us.

Swana. Seems like the Family will have better plans for Adam. Look at Sigi arguing, must be her headman.

After the search, Sigi lays down in bed crying in great addiction. Adam isn't around so she isn't pretending. Adam eventually arrives and notices Sigi is tormented and trying to hide it. She wipes her tears as Adam holds her and kisses her brow. He whispers 'I will take care of you no matter what'.

Orla. I don't believe she is acting so don't mislead her.

Adam. I am not. I can almost feel her pain.

Orla. Still, once she is a sleep make sure you quietly search your abode for anything alien.

Adam. What do you mean?

Orla. She might have searched your abode to find your frailties if any. But she could also implant something to frame you.

Adam. Is there an approbation for this?

Orla. I heard enough chatter about how far the Family will go. There are no boundaries when they are involved. I will ask around to see if any O viewed the orbs memorizer.

The Family's Os are still humans. They are more cunning than the SYN's yet they still operate in stealth wonderment of their subjects. Sigi stayed at Adam's abode for more nights and days and is now fascinated by him, her former high-value subjects exploited her beauty while she pledged loyalty to the Family. On the contrary, Adam was such an honorable gent with her since their first rendezvous and now more genuine and ardent with her. She feels genuinely cherished for the first time in a long time, she might be falling for him too quickly, a great sin that she wouldn't dare to confess. She can no longer look into Adam's eyes without a high level of moral culpability and just wants him to hold her tight instead. In the darkness of night, she would silently let go of a few tears, Adam would notice but wouldn't ask, he already understands.

Adam. I don't know what to make of this anymore. I am starting to feel for her. She is either too theatrical or too broken.

Orla. I heard she searched your abode and many Os believe she refused to entrap you. Her career is certainly over in such a case. Either way, I believe she is not pretending.

Adam. I feel sorry for her being in such a dilemma.

Orla. She could also be worried knowing something might happen to you. We need to be extra cautious Adam. She will not tell you as that will be the end of her.

Adam. I will be the same with her and everyone regardless. Enough Os her years vying within.

Orla. That's why I wondered if the patron wanted you to vie for the goodness in all of us. But I no longer believe, and I won't let you either. The Family has taken over and all I hope for is to save the one they lust for the most, you Adam.

Adam. I won't believe in such wickedness to be a necessity.

Orla. I forgot to ask Adam. I noticed you never mentioned your land.

Adam. There was never a need. I am who I am without it.

Orla. It must have defined your admirable character.

Adam. Some of it. But its flaws have taken over its pride.

Orla. Would you tell me anything about it?

Adam. Anything, what interests you?

Orla. Inhabitants' pride, topography, edibles.

Adam. It sounds like an insight the SYN would yen for.

Orla. I can feel your smile so I know you don't mean it.

Adam. Right, I forgot I can't pretend with you. Where shall I begin?

Orla. Anything you like.

Adam. Half of my land didn't endure the worldly war. I meant the SFV. The mountains shielded the other half, our half. Super lands would have needed to wipe all mountains but it have been neither effective nor valuable. My kinfolk moved to a gorge. The conurbation is no more and with it all our certitudes. We still have elders chatter though about our ancient pride, old dogma and our plain inhabitants. We still had elders chatter though of our ancient pride, old dogma and our plain inhabitants. Preceding the SFV, our land wasn't in good fettle with a major sparsity of coins. Our chosen servants weren't serving the land but their coins. Land turned pale but their abodes were glassy and green. Elders say super lands had a hand.

Orla. You sound bitter. Is that the reason you left your land?

Adam. How so? SFV reset us all. And I have no servant scheme. I belong to my adventures and my kinfolk. I never felt I belonged to that land. This is now my promised land, that until I finish dealing with the SYN.

Orla. You know Adam, your land preceding the SFV

reminds me of the Laman Hamlet's story. The Family might have had a hand in it all.

Adam. They might have, but all our certitudes vanished so no one knows for certain.

Orla. The Blau Family collected the rolls of all inhabitants and certitudes of all lands before the vying began. Certitudes none of the SYNs has.

Adam. So they own and can distort certitudes! That's too much power to have.

Orla. Exactly, the reason inhabitants believe their say, oppos fear their way and our servants take their pay.

Adam. Becoming a poet?

Orla. No, it's just a famous saying we have of the Family. What about your kinfolk? What about your kinfolk? To whom does the connotation M1 refer to?

Adam. I don't know yet.

Orla. You still don't trust me, I understand.

Adam. No I do. But it's only revealed at 22.

Orla. Seriously? Ours at 21, I will know mine this year.

Adam. What is Yours?

Orla. K49

Adam. Orla K49 I will remember it.

The meaning behind the Kinfolk's connotation is revealed at different ages based on the land's dictum. Sometimes an exception is given to certain kinfolks to make such a reveal at an even later age if they are important enough and don't trust youngsters of such a reveal. S34 has suffered enough since the SFV for its supposed resources and Adam could also be of great importance if his kinfolk has influence in such a Land. The Family might know of such importance from old rolls and are not revealing to the SYN of such worth. Still, a single letter proceeded by a single digit such as Adam M1 is enough to signal that his kinfolk are important enough to receive it before other kinfolks.

Needless to say, Land and kinfolks connotation has been crucial in eliminating pre-SFV stigma and protecting resources and affliction, it's; however, less discussed how most surviving and far lands blindly believed in this and more importantly agreed to it. Elder chatter did mention that the Family, having old rolls, encouraged such dictums as they covertly needed to eliminate the pride that comes from the rich history of said lands and kinfolks; as well as, influence future affairs by decoding the connotations without any disturbance from wannabe competitors.

THE TOUGH LIFE

Adam leaves his abode to find his bike missing. He was late to moiling but arrived to find another more upsetting news.

Adam. Did you see that? I just lost my post.

Orla. The way your gaffer has been trying to frame you for a while, now this accusation and quick investigation was a sham. They can't dismiss you with such a mere accusation. Such a poor excuse!

Adam. Are you thinking what I am thinking?

Orla. Yes, it could be SYN. They could have taken your bike too. I can't read your rolls and I doubt it would be written in them. Such disruption would be more of a favor for future coins.

Adam. Oh well. I don't feel like vying for such a post. I'll look for another one.

Orla. If it's them behind it there won't be another post.

Adam. What shall I do then? I can't be without coins!

Orla. That's what they are counting on. Let me help Adam.

Adam. We have talked about it. Please don't. I will figure it out.

Swana. He doesn't seem to be bothered by losing his post.

Anan. Not yet, he will be after a few closed doors.

Swana. How long is this going on for?? I hate his pride! I hate it!!

Anan. More jealous of him for being a freegent? Don't worry he won't be for long. Besides, you are moiling coins for watching an interesting show.

Swana. You mean an indolent show! I care about the coins but this is just going on forever and I need to live and entertain.

Anan. It is all interesting to me cause we haven't met anyone quite like Adam. He is a subject worth observing.

Swana. I admire your fascination but you need to live more. You are too comely to be alone.

Anan. I am neither alone nor lonely.

Swana. Keep telling yourself that. No one seems to know your private affairs aside from the SYN's collateral of you.

Anan. Life moil concinnity. I know where and when to draw the line.

Swana. Does this cross the line...

Anan. What are you doing? Not again Swana...just stop it.

Swana. Just relax for a minute. Don't Sweat it, I keep all my affairs private too ... including you.

Anan. Just this time then be obliging with the deputation.

Swana. I promise.

Finally, Swana seduced Anan. He denied his loneliness but all Os roam in the same crowded tunnel; yet, it's too dark inside to see or feel anything hence they still need validation from time to time. It isn't Amour, just a distrustful flimsy distraction to fritter away time.

Adam was across the road and stopped for a moment before opening the door to his abode. He must be thinking of his kinfolk and the lack of coins he wanted to concede for them. He might be good at hiding it but his old dogma always prevails in calamities.

Sigi. You are back. How was your day?

Orla. She must know about it. She doesn't look alright.

Adam. It was fine.

Sigi. You seem down. What happened?

Adam. Nothing important but I lost my post.

Sigi. Oh Dear Adam, let me come closer... I am confident you will find something better. Just show them this lovely smile in the next confabulation.

Adam. I am not worried. Plus I now have more time to spend with you.

Sigi. Have you thought of an autarchy? moiling your own coins?

Adam. I have, it takes time and coins to survive its journey.

Sigi. You have been great to me Adam. I don't have much coins but I have enough for both of us to live off. Let me take care of our tally and you focus on an autarchy.

Adam. I can't a..

Orla. Adam Wait! Accept it!

Adam. I can’t Orla!

Sigi. I eagerly want to help and might be a great adventure for both of us.

Orla. Say yes, I will explain. Plus she's got enough coins.

Adam. I don't know what to say to you Sigi.

Sigi. Say yes.

Adam. I am glad I met you Sigi.

Sigi. Is that a yes?

Adam. I can't say no to you unless those eyes allow me to.

Sigi. No, you are never allowed to say no to me. Now kiss me.

Orla. Oh not again!

Adam. That's your fault. Later Orla

Swana. Did you just hear that trull!? She is wrecking our plan!

Anan. She isn't supposed to offer him coins. The patron won't be thrilled.

Swana. Is the Family fine with it? Nothing we can do if so... as usual.

Anan. I doubt but they have their ways. The patron needs to face them this time.

Swana. Poor Anan... You still believe in SYN's USS over the Family.

Anan. Let's not pass judgment until we know what Sigi's plan is. We can only follow our instructions and watch everything play.

That's an unexpected oppo move by Sigi and Orla. Os hide having coins so they can't offer them even when trying to gain the trust of subjects. Sigi must have a zero-sum game or a costly attachment to Adam. Orla must have a plan of her own as this is out of her character. Nothing linked to Adam is ordinary and all this will prolong his deputation even more for a mere fascination.

Adam. She is asleep. She seems happy and not pretending. Can you now indulge me why I was forced to accept her offer knowing it's out of my character?

Orla. I won't prettify it Adam, the SYN must want to drain you. This tactic is cruel and lasts for as long as it takes. You will need coins from wherever you can have them. Sigi is a member of the Family, but even she isn't allowed to offer them. Regardless of the reason she offered you coins, take the help. I do feel she genuinely wants to help you and she might even convince the Family of her logic.

Adam. How can the SYN get away with all of this! This is about the inhabitant's livelihood! So vicious !!

Orla. Now you understand why I am with you Adam. I used to believe it was all a necessary evil. Now I know it's not necessary, just evil.

Adam. She is up later

Orla. Later.

Sigi. Adam there is a nice new place for edibles, let's go try it.

Adam. You know I don't have enough coins.

Sigi. Adam!... We agreed.

Adam. Ok you decide.

Sigi. Of course, I will decide. I don't trust your taste.

Adam. My taste in damsels right? I have no choice as you know. So enjoy your superiority until I make my own coins then I will spoil you.

Sigi. Fine Mr. Coins. Tell me, how can we make autarchy a reality?

Adam. I don't want you to take more risk for me than you have to. The Family must be worried.

Sigi. What do you mean by the Family?..

Orla. Adam!!

Adam. I meant your kinfolk. How can you explain giving your coins to a stranger?

Sigi. Don't worry about it Adam. Plus I already spoke to them about you.

Adam. and...

Sigi. They seem to like the idea of you but they don't fully understand your land and kinfolk and that worries them.

Adam. Such a cliche. Can't I be different?

Sigi. I know you are but I need to explain it all to them.

Adam. Since they won't approve of me, I must meet them.

Orla. What are you doing Adam?!

Sigi. I don't know Adam. It's hard and they are in another land currently.

Adam. You sound hesitant.

Sigi. No not at all. We just can't move things that fast.

Adam. As you wish.

Sigi. If it was up to me I would move mountains for you. And although I truly trust you I won't be totally honest with you. I wish I could explain the situation with my kinfolk but I know I can't be totally honest with you. You deserve someone better. This is the first I have even this honest.

Orla. I can't believe both of you! She might have understood your suspicion. And she is giving you enough honesty although not directly. You are both lucky to be having edibles away from the SYN's orbs !!

Adam. Don't ever lose this soul Sigi. You are more beauteous on the inside than anyone would realize.

Sigi. Do you mean I am not as beauteous from the outside?

Adam. Now you understand how hard it is for me to be with you if it wasn't for your coins.

Sigi. Such an an entanglement.

Adam. Seriously... You are fetching and your soul is now elegantly shining and making you gorgeous. Never lose that soul.

Sigi. I wish I can promise but I promise to do all I can.

Adam. That's enough for me.

Orla. Are you falling for her? Just remember she has a long history that might haunt her sleep and yours.

Adam. Is someone jealous Orla?,

Orla. I care about you Adam but not like that. I promised to protect you. Even if she means well, she will be a heavy weight to carry.

Adam. I will try to save one soul like you are saving mine. If we all save one, the SYN and Family will run out of fresh souls to take.

Orla. It's easier with an inhabitant like you Adam. She has seen and done things she can't undo.

Adam. I will still not give up on her.

Orla. Then I will do my best to help you both.

Adam. That's my Orla!

She wishes she could reply that that's my Adam but Orla can not admit to him or anyone of her feelings. Os are afraid of the SYN's hand in such personal affairs, it's even fatal to be with Adam. If you amour someone, walk to another land for their well-being. Orla sympathized with Sigi but didn't expect all of this, no one did.

Sigi. So what's your plan for the autarchy?

Adam. I am thinking of what this land lacks. Something pure that inhabitants can't ignore.

Sigi. Not much is left pure after the SFV.

Adam. Who's fault do you think?

Sigi. I don't know. Perished knowledge, Greed?

Orla. Don't try Adam, she wouldn't dare mention the Family.

Adam. She said enough, I'll give her that.

Adam. Tell me Sigi, do you believe in me making coins uninterrupted with a pure delicacy?

Sigi. With those eyes? I will buy anything you're selling. Anything in your Pate?

Adam. S34's mountains have enough yields. I will think of something to daze this land of pre-SFV joy.

Sigi. I am excited for this journey!

There is no pre-SFV joy that the Family can't deploy or won't destroy if it isn't in their coins' interest. Poor Adam, he believes in the land's dictums to protect his dreams. Losing a post isn't the only trick inside the SYN's hat. His every dream can become foggy while he continues in his sleep. If that dream touches the Family's interest or coins no matter how small, that dream will become an everlasting nightmare and no dictums or USS can wake him up to such a reality.

Orla. The Family seems to approve Sigi's gifts.

Adam. Do you mean it's all planned? How did you know?

Orla. Orbs. She discussed it in your abode. She knows the SYN will hear it.

Adam. Another trap?

Orla. Not necessarily. She could've wanted to explain her actions. She must have been convincing.

Adam. Oh Sigi... I have nothing to lose I presume.

Orla. No choice either.

Adam. We will let it play and I will do all I can to make it a success.

Orla. I am always with you.

Adam. That's my only hope.

THE AUTARCHY

Sigi. Have we decided Mr. Adam?

Adam. Yes, Honey!

Sigi. Such an ancient vocable. Pure?

Adam. Yes, Pure.

Sigi. Didn't all the bees die?

Adam. They survived in our mountains.

Sigi. How come no one heard of this?

Adam. It has been secretly reserved for our inhabitants.

Little did Adam realize that such news could be the end of their pure joy. The Family loves to take everything over and make it theirs. At first, honey will flourish but it will never stay pure. Those who have no soul only flourish with seduction, not pure.

Adam starts to receive pure honey and it dazed inhabitants. Pure honey has not been savoured for almost 6 decades. Even the Family with their coins weren't aware of its existence. Soon enough, Adam was becoming famed among F3 inhabitants. A gent resampling hope moiling honorable coins his own way. This is a threat to the SYN's obedience scheme. The Family might want him to succeed so they can take it over but the SYN wants him to fail so the idea of a free soul is over.

While promoting his honey, an elder gent stopped by Adam's trading post to hear him passionately promote his honey. He seems in his later years but sharp and healthy with a shaved beard and mustache, wearing a casual yet exorbitant spring garb. His name was Wise and seemed amazed by Adam's knowledge of honey, its variety and colors.

Wise. I haven't seen a more passionate gent like you in ages. What's your name?

Adam. I am Adam. And honored to meet you. Have you heard of our honey Mr?

Wise. Mr. Wise. Negative... I am intrigued to know all about it if I may. I can sense your excitement, what makes it so special?

Adam. It's pure. Nothing like it in all the far lands.

Wise. Mr. Adam, I am old enough to have tasted pure honey. There is rarely anything pure anymore... certainly not the delicacy of pure honey since bees didn't survive the SFV.

Adam. I am now more excited for you to try it to believe it.

Wise. I will have the darker colored one, the look reminds me of the colour of honey I used to savour as a youngster. How many coins?

Adam. No coins for trying. It will be a pleasure seeing a smile of happy memories.

Wise. I insist Mr. Adam. Take those coins.. I desire to support those seeking to moil for their own coins.... Oh my lord, this is pure! How did you find such a delicacy?

Adam. I didn't find it. Our mountains and inhabitants preserved it.

Wise. Mr. Adam. You have made me a happy elder gent and I haven't had such a smile in a while. I am contemplating giving you an offer, … as a matter of fact, I am confident that I should. I will make you a gent of valuable coins and a worthy status in this land. An offer that will make you, your kinfolk and all the inhabitants in your land rejoice.

Adam. I don't fully understand.. What kind of offer?

Wise. I want to acquire the majority of your autarchy for valuable coins but you get to steer the autarchy for me. I will make sure this honey flourishes from your land to all surviving and far lands. You and your name will be celebrated across all of them.

Adam. I sincerely thank you for such an offer Mr. Wise but I am only interested in keeping our honey pure and it can only continue as such if bees and old ways remain the same. I also want the freedom to make choices without impacting anyone's livelihood or your coins.

Wise. Mr. Adam, you might not be aware but I can assure you that in order to make it far in our land you need to moil for someone bigger than your dreams. It's just the way it is.

Adam. I will keep that in mind Mr. Wise and I appreciate the offer.

Wise. Remember my offer Mr. Adam there might still be time to take it but not long enough. Until then enjoy the excitement.

Adam. Orla ... You have been quiet have I bored you with my autarchy?

Orla. No Adam, I am thrilled for you and learning your style in pleasuring emptors.

Adam. Not everyone seemed thrilled and I meant to ask you about the last emptor, Mr. Wise. What do you make of him?

Orla. I meant to tell you I recognize him but I don't remember from where?

Adam. The SYN?

Orla. Not that I know of. He doesn't seem the type with such confidence… He is aged far beyond someone like me to know of him.

Adam. Something about what he said to me and the way he said it wasn't to be neglected.

Orla. Adam! I remember him! He was once in a chatter with the Patron... It seemed like a serious chatter in the park that I interrupted. I remember asking the Patron who he was and he said, no one important.

Adam. He seems important enough to have such coins. You must be sharing my discernment.

Orla. A member of the Family?

Adam. Indeed. Seems like a senior member. I thought of it when he mentioned the offer... The Hamlet's affair ran through my pate!

Orla. Oh dear Adam. If he is and they aren't happy with such rejection then expect tricks beyond my training and knowledge. I will keep an eye on the SYN's rolls for any requests. I still doubt they will be mentioned.

Adam. Have no fear Orla. I am to expect and accept all that comes my way without such fear. I am just glad you are with me.

Orla. Wish we could live without such thoughts and fated truth. I am always with you, come what may.

These two could have not been in more misfortune. Not only are they distended to stay apart and invisible but also face both the SYN and Family as nemeses. A mental challenge few can endure and survive. Mr. Wise is indeed an active elder of the Family, still excited to wake up for coins like a young gent vying for amour and now feels as though Adam is stealing that amour and thrill away from him. It won't be long before Adam feels the invisible wrath of the Family using the SYN's might.

Adam. Did you just witness this?

Orla. I did they were brash, I am sorry Adam.

Adam. Never be. You don't represent all the wrongs in this land or the SYN's. This is just the third time my honey was spurned. How can this be when inhabitants thirst for it?

Orla. We both know why Adam.

Adam. I just wish I had corroboration.

Orla. It will be hard Adam. Even if you have corroboration, Dictums don't supersede USS and USS thwart Judges, a vicious circle of squandered years, your years.

Adam. It was meant to be as such, wasn't it?

Orla. The old hopper of me would have disagreed but I now believe it was meant to be this way. A mere show of hope ...

Adam. What USS is being used for this?

Orla. I wouldn't know, they will twist one for you and actuate a deputation unchallenged.

Adam. This is so unfair.. not just to me but to such a beauteous land and inhabitants.

Orla. Inhabitants don't feel this. But I hear you... I feel you.

Adam's pure honey was repudiated by most pedlars after being dazed. Some even squandered this ancient delicacy in front of Adam making it clear that he and his honey are lamentable. The sudden repudiation wasn't a coincidence. The SYN and Family had enough of Adam's autarchy, some Os are looking up to him while others grumble about his success. More importantly, the Family had observed enough.

The sumptuous life the Family supports provides inhabitants with soulless seduction. A seductive affair tied with coins and vanished with them. Inhabitants aren't to feel thus not to complain when moiling for their coins. Woefully for Adam, he gets to feel but not to heal. He no longer gets to moil coins and nowhere to grumble. Having corroboration wouldn't have assisted him having no courageous defenders on this land to represent him. On the contrary, it could make him a visible foe of the SYN, and the SYN will frame him as a foe of the land.

Sigi. Welcome back Adam.

Adam. Thanks Sigi .... Aren't you going to ask me?

Sigi. About?

Adam. My day and autarchy.

Sigi. I meant to, you seem fine and I am confident your autarchy will be a success. You are a savvy gent.

Orla. She knows the autarchy adventure is almost over, she seems sad so don't do this to her.

Adam. Oh dear Sigi ... I don't know if I am any good at this. Every gate I need to go through is guarded. I shouldn't have promised you.

Sigi. Don't you ever give up Adam... Adam, I need to tell you something.

Adam. I am listening.

Sigi. I don't think this is working between us... I am falling for another gent,.. I just couldn't tell you.

Adam. What? When did that happen?

Sigi. You were busy with the autarchy so I didn't want to be a bothersome.

Adam. Do I get a chance to mend whatever pain I might have caused?

Sigi. You didn't cause any. I just believe this is better for all of us.

Orla. I don't like the timing of this Adam!

Adam. Me neither.

Adam. Why now Sigi?

Sigi. I don't feel that we are truly together. Please understand.

Orla. She won't be honest with you... Let her go Adam.

Adam. Orla ... I need to know first what will happen next.

Adam. As you desire Sigi. I just wish I had more coins to take care of you. Thanks for everything and hopefully one day I can return the favor.

Orla. She has enough coins, worry about yourself going forward.

Sigi. Can I stay here one last night?

Adam. No need to ask, this is your abode too.

Sigi. I appreciate it all. I am late for my new gent, will see you later tonight.

Adam. Seriously Orla why is she doing this?

Orla. She is obviously forced to do this. I believe she likes you. She wouldn't do this to you unless she had no choice.

Adam. Do you think she is in menace? Was it her wish or am I in menace?

Orla. With all that is going on to you, this actually makes sense and is just a continuation. It happens separately so no one can connect them all but you. The post, the autarchy and the amour all perished with Zephyr.

Adam. Am I next?

Orla. There would be nothing to gain, so don't entertain such thoughts, they need you in such a stage for something. I need to read all your rolls! Now it's urgent.

Adam. Don't Orla.. they might find out.

Orla. This is critical Adam. I can't predict their next moves and I promised to protect you. Even if I don't make it, I will still sacrifice it all for you.

Adam. No, I forbid you from making such a sacrifice.... You know what Orla ... if there is one last sacrifice to make for me it would be something else.

Orla. Anything for you Adam, anything!

Adam. I want to see you! If nothing happens to you but everything to me then it will at least be worth it.

Orla. It would be worth it for me too... we shall finally meet then, We just can't be seen together that's all.

Adam. So we now have our little deputation?

Orla. The most exciting deputation, my heart is racing already.

Adam. You might feel mine, no need to tell you.

Orla. Tranquility Adam ...I might actually hear it.

Adam. Your inner voice has always made it beat peacefully. You just made it race and I won't complain.

Swana. What the tophet did just happen?

Anan. You mean Sigi?

Swana. Yes! Why is she leaving like this?

Anan. The Family and patron continue the plan to hammer Adam.

Swana. Not like this! Sigi will be exposed, her departure isn't believable. We never leave like this even when breaking hearts.

Anan. You are overreacting. Why do you even care?

Swana. I have been in such deputations enough times to

know how she feels right now.

Anan. Her feelings are irrelevant.

Swana. Maybe to you but to us, after all the theatrics and degradation, we need to leave knowing we made a believable valuable contribution or at least depart unexposed!

Anan. She is experienced enough and will get over this.

Swana. No one can prepare us for such a departure. I just hope she remembers her worth. Poor Sigi!

Anan. Now that she is out of play we need to keep our eyes wide open. Adam's reaction has to be carefully analyzed.

Swana. I hate this deputation.

Anan. Don't take me and our little fun for granted or I shall report you.

Swana. You will be giving me a gift. I don't ever want to be another Sigi.

Anan. Take this beverage it will help you relax. Remember we are here to help each other.

Swana. Take your hand off me Anan. I mean it! I need time alone.

Anan. Fine take your time and I will watch Adam. Be ready to take over soon or all of this will be in your rolls.

Although indirectly, it's apparent that Adam's influence over Os is becoming contagious. Swana's feelings for Sigi could have a pernicious effect on the SYN's future. The SYN and, more frequently, the Family have tools and ways learned from vanished super lands; Still, soft power such as Sigi's is the bridge to all closed castles and treasures. Such a bridge over-lasted wars and said castles and will isolate and over-last the SYN if it fails to protect it. Adam's deputation is creating a crack in that bridge.

Adam. Good morning beauteous damsel.

Orla. Who are you talking to? I thought Sigi was gone.

Adam. Who else can hear my pate and talk to my heart?

Orla. You have never met me, you can take it back until we meet. Seeing me might make you change your mind.

Adam. Your beauteous mind, soul, inner voice and deeds are hard to be overshadowed by anything else.

Orla. Are you sure you still want to see me?

Adam. I would never say no to Elysium.

Orla. Sounds like a final place.

Adam. I meant eternal happiness.

Orla. Your land still believes in such hope. We have lost it.

Adam. F3 is beauteous Orla, if not for being crippled by the SYN and Family.

Orla. I am trying to forget them for the first time with you.

Adam. My fault. I will make you forget every pain and sorrow. Is little deputation ready?

Orla. I think I have an idea. But nothing for definite. You are the most-watched subject, especially after sigi.

Adam. How is she doing if I may ask.

Orla. You may ask and I may decline to remind you of her.

Adam. She didn't feel right when leaving. I do care about her just not in the way I care about you.

Orla. She took time to herself. I believe that's a good sign.

Adam. Good to hear. Kindly keep me informed.

Orla. I will... just not in the tryst, the tryst is mine!

Adam. The tryst is yours, but you are mine...

THE TRYST

Orla. Good daybreak fine gent.

Adam. An excellent one hearing such a beauteous mind.

Orla. Do you hear my excited mind?

Adam. You have a plan?!

Orla. I believe I do. I finally can put my knowledge into an exciting deputation.

Adam. I guess assisting me all this time wasn't exciting.

Orla. Adam please, that was charity but this Tryst is mine, don't forget.

Adam. Charity? I didn't know I was adopted by you. You know I could've been spoiled by Sigi instead.

Orla. You really had to bring her into this.

Adam. With all seriousness, I am thrilled and listening, Continue…

Orla. I am nervous but I believe it will work. You must have orbs in every zone in your abode and once you step out you will be followed too. You have to be in another closed area attending an invite-only event which I will be sending you, we will then have a few minutes to ourselves.

Adam. It's exciting but not amorous. I want to make you the happiest damsel.

Orla. I will be happy to meet you anywhere, even on the edge of a cliff and jump with you if they come for us. I just don't want this to be our first and last amorous rendezvous. Do you?

Adam. That depends on how beauteous you are.

Orla. Really?

Adam. Bantering with you is more charming than all the damsels I have met. Now tell me, wouldn't the SYN find a way to get invited?

Orla. They invite themselves everywhere and all the time. The trick is they do not know of it in advance, they always have a plan or at least a prediction but they hate surprises.

Adam. I am assuming they go through my travelbags.

Orla. They do but I doubt they will expect it unless they believe you are going.

Adam. I have an idea... Send me an invite to a closed event that requires coins which I am obviously not willing to pay for and I will even neglect to open the invite until the hour.

Orla. Consider it done.

Adam. One more thing. Make sure there is a back door. I will take it over from there.

Orla. Where are we going after?

Adam. I am glad you can't read my mind. I will turn the amorous rendezvous into a wild escapade.

Orla. I wish you can see my smile.

Adam. I will see it and feel it when we meet. Oh I forgot.

Orla. What?

Adam. Can you bring me some habiliment so we can walk out unrecognized?

Orla. I already have that in mind.

Adam. A blind tryst for me with someone who knows me and choosing my habiliment. This is all new to me.

Unlike the SYN, these two have started a moral and legitimate little deputation and it seems to become a reality. Few Os have ever revealed themselves to subjects without subjects becoming Os. This is an oceanic show of trust and amour by Orla. She was able to convince her masseur to send Adam an invite to a one hour splurgy session for large coins. She also convinced her to pretend to attend to Adam while the two leave using the back door which is reserved for them. The little amorous deputation will begin before sunset in two nights.

Orla. It's time Adam.

Adam. Are you sure you want to do this? Once I see you it can't be undone.

Orla. If you are sure you want to see me then all my worries will be gone.

Adam. There is nothing I am sure of more than being with you at the edge of that cliff ready to jump.

Orla. I am ready Adam too.

Adam. Let's do it!

After grabbing a beverage and meandering around the abode wearing a resting garment, Adam noticed the unopened invitation on top of the entrance cedenza. He opens it to read the invitation and scrambles to wear his attire and walks to the door.

Anan. What was in the letter Swana?

Swana. He didn't receive any important ones!

Anan. Whatever it was, it made him move. Let's leave.

Swana. I am not feeling it. You go.

Anan. Apologies I forgot you only move to bassinets.

Swana. Just leave me alone already.

Adam leaves the abode rushing to his unscheduled Tryst. He was hoping to evade Anan and Swana but Anan was quick enough to follow him. Orla was watching from a distance.

Orla. He is following you Adam. Keep the theatrics.

Adam. I was hoping he wasn't, no worries.

Orla. My masseur has everything prepared.

Adam. Everything? And I was hoping for some surprises.

Orla. Let's fuddle Anan first. Now take the first right it will be the door in blue but act like you aren't sure.

Adam. I will but I won't hide my excitement.

Orla. Adam.. My heart is racing and you bantering?

Adam. I arrived. I am going in.

Anan continues to follow Adam not knowing what he is up to. He goes through the same door in a rush then takes a few steps back as Adam is right in front of him talking to the receiver. He steps outside quietly to see the sign for a masseur. Anan inserts an aural contraption into his right ear that is barely visible and sends a signal to Swana.

Anan. Did he receive anything from a masseur?

Swana. He did but it was splurgy, I didn't think he would go for it.

Anan. He did and we are now unprepared. I can't faze anyone here not knowing their rolls and I can't stand inside or have a masseur in case he leaves, and I hate waiting outside, its beginning to rain.... such a daunting day!

Swana. The reason I prefer bassinets.

Anan. Why am I even signaling to you! I'll just hack it alone.

Adam is led to a private room and Anan steps in again to see where he was headed. The receiver looks at Anan 'Greeting gent, a pleasure awaits you'. 'I wasn't in any slot, any available?' he asked. She then replied 'Your fortuitous day indeed we have, span?' 'suggestion?' Anan requested. 'That depends on your eunoia' she replied with a smile. Anan responded with a fake smirk ' That will require days then.. Actually, the gent that just got in what did he elect? 'an hour' she responded. 'May I see the amenity'. She then took him to an empty room that was a few ones across from Adam's which wouldn't help him hear Adam leaving. On his way to the exit he abruptly opened Adam's room to see Adam already lying and facing down. He apologized for intruding and the masseur went to lock the door. Anan apologized to the receiver feigning no tendency towards the rooms and was hoping Adam's would be different. He then leaves and waits outside across the road from the front door feeling and hating every drop of rain on his face and shoulders and hating the reason he has to get wet while Adam is getting a massage. In reality, he hates being oblivious to the actual reason for this travail deputation and being in this situation despite his years of exceptional moil for the SYN.

Adam continued to receive a massage when the masseur said she would step out for a moment. Adam then asks Orla.

Adam. Is it now should I get dressed?

Orla. Not now. I have a surprise for you.

Suddenly someone walks into the room and he feels hands on his back robbing gently. His heart started racing. 'Is that you?' Adam says it in a peaceful way.

Orla. How does it feel?

Adam. Let me turn.

Orla. No wait! Anan might pass by. Tell me.

Adam. Your hands know their ways. Anything you want to tell me?

Orla. How would you know? Anything you want to tell me?

Adam. I am turning... This isn't you. I knew it.

Orla. How would you know? I am just a voice in your head. Turn back please.

Adam. I have painted a picture of you in my pate. This isn't it.

Orla. What if I am not the damsel in your pate? Would be such a disappointment. Still want to do this?

Adam. Now more than ever...

Orla. Then take the bag by the entrance it has your habiliment. The masseur will show you the back door. I will keep an eye on Anan while you leave.

Adam thanked the masseur, got ready and smoothly left from the back door.

Adam. It's raining.

Orla. I forgot to bring us a gamp!

Adam. No need, I have a fondness for the rain.

Orla. Me too... Not the reason I didn't bring any.

Adam. I will walk to the cafe in the corner and leave from the other entrance to make sure no one is tagging me.

Orla. Clever, I don't see Swana so I am a little worried.

Adam. I want to see you but I don't want it to be the last time please be careful.

Orla. I will watch from a distance in case she is around.

Swana has left the building but she is nowhere to be found in the area and rarely replies to Anan's inessential queries. While Adam enters the cafe, Orla closes her eyes to see where he is heading. She can only see through his eyes when hers are closed. She keeps opening them to see if anyone resembling an O is entering and closes them to see what Adam is seeing and his location. She then takes faster steps to follow Adam from the opposite entrance but then loses track of him. He seemed to look into a brick wall but then closed his eyes.

Orla. Where are you Adam? I can't tell.

Adam. Just continue walking.

Orla. What do you mean? I don't see you or through you.

Adam. I know where you are, continue…

She continues not knowing where Adam is for the first time. But Adam can hear the steps of an elegant damsel not seeking attention yet he kept his eyes closed making it impossible for Orla to know where he is. She then suddenly hears someone walking behind her and before she can turn, two hands covere her eyes to make her heart come close to a stop.

Orla. Tell me this is you.

Adam. Yes

Orla. Then open your eyes...

Something special just happened for Adam. Orla actually opened her lips to say those vocables for Adam to finally hear her serene voice for the first time. Adam opened his eyes to see the back of her luxuriant smooth auburn hair in front of him with a fading lavender smell blended with the smell of the rain before closing his eyes again. He opened his lips and told her 'I will lead you, just trust me'. This was Orla's first time hearing his dulcet caring voice with her own ears and her first time not seeing though his eyes. More importantly, his first time leading her while she is the one fully trusting him. They kept their eyes closed carefree of any O that could be around. This is their empyrean and the SYN won't be allowed to enter it.

Orla. Where are we going Adam?

Adam. A place I have always wanted to be with you.

Adam continues leading her while they are both seeing nothing expect enjoying each others voices and feeling the drizzle. He knew every turn, warning her of every step just like she used to warn him. They both didn't mind getting lost in the rain. The roads had nothing and no one moving because of it. Nothing to disrupt their amorous walk.

Adam then asked her to keep her eyes closed and hop on his back as he carry's her down a nature-made staircase leading behind a cascade to a small cave covered by the small falls. He then stopped, gently let her of his back and asked her to keep her eyes closed. He then moved to face her.

Adam. Keep your eyes closed.

Orla. That's not fair...

Adam. It was never fair for me all this time.

He then opened his eyes to see Orla's sublime beauty for the first time with a Radiant smile and the luxuriant auburn hair.

Adam. I hope you can appreciate how resplendent you are through my eyes.

He then gave her a decorous kiss in her pate. She opened her eyes for him to gaze at her Seraphic green eyes.

Orla. Hello Adam.

Adam. Hello Orla.

Orla. This was long overdue.

Adam. Indeed Orla, Indeed.

She then hugged him and he kissed her hair. They both said nothing for a minute. Just a genuine embrace when vocables weren't needed to paint their feelings. A moment many would dream of but only they deserved. Adam then wondered if she was tired.

Adam. I have only been here a couple of times. I remember there was no were comfy to set on. I didn't want to ask you to carry anything. Are you fatigued? cold?

Orla. No I am used to being wet under the rain, it cleanses my worries away. This is a beauteous hidden place Adam. I feel free... with you Adam I feel free.

They sat beside each others on the muddy rocky surface and she didn't mind it while wearing a tailored green bodycon dress that matched her eyes. They both smiled while gazing at each others eyes almost matching colors.

Orla. Finally.

Adam. Fanciful.

Orla. Was I as envisioned?

Adam. I couldn't have possibly imagined a pulchritudinous redhead with such Elysian eyes.

Orla. What did you imagine?

Adam. A Burnett for some reason.

Orla. You never asked.

Adam. You wouldn't have told me.

Orla. Saddened?

Adam. On the contrary, I am enchanted by it. We just don't have redheads in our mountains and rarely have I seen any here.

Orla. It's auburn.

Adam. Right, I now need to learn all the shades of redheads in case I meet others.

Orla. That won't happen!

Adam. Should I be worried?

Orla. A little...

Adam. Needless to ask how you envisioned me. You know me well.

Orla. Still, I haven't met such a debonair gent with a tranquil gaze. Plus, you don't take time to look at yourself in the mirror... For me at least...

Adam. I couldn't, knowing you were watching the same mirror with me. It's getting dark inside. Let's walk downstream, there is a small lake. Want to swim?

Orla. But I didn't bring a maillot. I hope you didn't expect me to take off any of this. I am not one of those damsels Adam.

Adam. I wouldn't want you to be otherwise. Can you jump in with the bodycon?

Orla. You know what? I will!

And they did, with such carefree laughter and happiness under the rain. There are those who enjoy a carefree life under the rain and those who cover up and feeling every drop as a stain. These two are of the former, with no theatrics in such a first tryst for they have known each other for what feels like an eternity. Lucky for them inhabitants were again no were to be found. Adam planned to just visit the Cave which wasn't far from the riddle bridge but since only a handful ever wandered to it like him, he also decided to go for a swim.

Adam must have ascertained that F3 inhabitants are too occupied paying their dues to take a risk and accidentally discover a jollity that could prevent them from paying such dues thus they continue with their lives not noticing the Os lying to their faces, let alone discover an entrance to a cave underneath them covered by a cascade. Adam; however, is adventurous having been raised on top of mountains. He took a risk leaving all behind to be in F3. Discovering its prettiness is the littlest risk he has ever taken.

Inhabitants do view the lake but never go in for a swim believing it could be contaminated after the SFV. A rummer the Family spread to solely profit from its rich minerals, forcing inhabitants to rely on the Family's water supply instead. Orla couldn't care of any supposed danger and was having a pleasant splashy time with Adam. He carried her to look again at her seraphic eyes.

Adam. I am finally at peace looking at your elysian eyes. You must be cold by now let's flame some branches in the cave.

Orla. You know how?

Adam. We often use flames in our mountains in the darkness of night.

Orla. I won't ask you with whom you did.

Adam. No one is as serene that's for sure. Can you help me choose some branches? I need at least one dry.

They both continue with their Amorous peaceful deputation without any care given if the whole land is burning. But an inhabitant was indeed burning from within.

Not far from the cave, Swana was promenading to gather her thoughts and started crossing the riddle bridge. She didn't know what to expect at such a dark hour. Maybe a gent and a one pleasurable night to ease her resentment only to find a damsel instead. The damsel was standing on top of the handrail in the middle of the riddle bridge. Swana couldn't reckon if that was a theatrics but there was no one else passing by to witness it. Swana then recognized the damsel, it was Sigi. She panicked and blustered at her.

Swana. SIGI STOP!!

Sigi. Swana? ...KEEP A DISTANCE SWANA!!

Swana. Whatever you think of doing don't. Remember who you are. Remember you are a member of the Family, your bright future is sealed.

Sigi. What bright future? The one full of theatrics, lies and deception? Aren't you tired of all the betrayals and secrets engraved in our skin? Twisting innocent subjects' fate without being given a reason? And for what? THRILL & COINS !!

Swana. FEAR! SIGI, FEAR!! ... Fear of what the SYN will do to me. Fear of losing my coins and no one taking care of me. Fear of a dark meaningless future. You wouldn't understand all this being a member the of Family. Now come down.

Sigi. Stand there SWANA! I am Serious!!

Swana. Alright... I hear you Sigi but why now? It's Adam, isn't it?

Sigi. He is real and pure Swana ... I wish you could understand how he made me feel for the first time in my life and I can't be with him.

Swana. You can when he joins us... be patient.

Sigi. I am not worth it. And he will never moil for the SYN. Besides, it's too late, his heart is already with her. I saw them, I know it's real.

Swana. Her? What's your chatter about? he isn't with anyone.

Sigi. So you don't know. More reason to know it's real.

Swana. The way you had to depart him was uncalled for and I felt your tears. I know the feeling Sigi, I am furious too.

Sigi. I suppose you would understand. We both had enough gents but you haven't been with Adam. Lucky for him, he fell for someone better than both of us. Lucky for Orla too.

Swana. Our Orla? The decent one? How? When?

Sigi. Promise me to let them be Swana. Let this be our sincere secret for goodness sake.

Swana. You know I can't do this Sigi. But we can both think of something. Just come down to chat.

Sigi. The SYN is always first isn't it? Or are you just afraid of losing your coins? I am done with them and our Family, the cruel Family that justifies it all for a greedy aim.

Swana. No, I am not anymore just don't DON'T SIGI NOOOO !! SIGIII NOOO ... SIGIII !! SIGIII !! What have I done!! I MEANT TO PROMISE YOU!! ... Sigi my dear Sigi . I promise I promise just stay alive. I will get help.

Swana was trained for the unexpected but never expected such a tragedy. She signaled to Anan who was calm as usual to listen. He then namelessly tipped off the Rozzers of an incident so they could rush to the river. The river current was too strong for sigi to swim for it even if she survived the fall.

Not far from the incident, Adam and Orla amble back to the main road above the Cave holding hands before deciding it would be safer to take different roads back not knowing if any Os were around. Adam will receive the unfortunate news the following midday.

Orla. Adam.

Adam. Yes darling, how was your night?

Orla. I had a wonderful one thanks to you.

Adam. You sound different. Did something happen or did I do anything? I hope you didn't catch a cold, it's all my fault.

Orla. I didn't want to bother you but I have some news.

Adam. Go on. I am all yours

Orla. I don't know how to say this. But there has been a tragedy at the Riddle Bridge.

Before Orla could continue, someone knocked on Adam's door. Adam goes to open it only to find the Rozzers standing. He never had to deal with them before and was surprised. They asked him for permission to enter although they didn't need any. They came prepared one after the other but one seemed in charge. He asked Adam.' We would like your assistance in answering some questions for the Land. 'Anything for the Land' Adam replied. 'Do you know a damsel named Sigi?' 'I did is she fine?'Adam asked hesitantly after

Orla's mention of a tragedy' We don't know yet and we were hoping you can tell us of the last time you were with her. Has she told you anything out of the ordinary, was she forlorn?' Adam responded with a worried tune. 'She seemed to have mixed feelings about a private matter that she didn't share with me. Can you kindly confirm if she is fine?' I will be honest Mr. Adam. A witness saw her jump off the riddle bridge. Although we can't confirm yet, this happens often at that bridge to assume that it is the truth. We confirmed that you were at a masseur's room so we are here hoping for any information that could help us understand her eunoia at the time'.

Orla. Adam, don't mention anything.

Adam. She deserves to be avenged!

Orla. I feel you but we won't be able to prove their doing if any. They have Os as Rozzers so taking such a risk will be a waste and a danger to you and me.

Rozzer. Mr. Adam? I know you are in shock and I see your tears. But if you know anything of value now is the time or the case will be closed like all the others at the Riddle Bridge.

Adam. All I know is she had a wonderful soul and I will miss her dearly.

Rozzer. I am sure she was. This concludes our case. Take care Mr. Adam.

Orla. I am so sorry Adam. I know you cared about her and I am in shock too. I didn't know she could take this road, especially as a member of the Family.

Adam. Did someone do this to her and don't you lie to me.

Orla. No one would dare do this to a member of the Family, the Family may do it to others but none would do it to them and there was no reason to. If it happened then it must be of free well. I will look into any rolls mentioning her.

Adam had bitter tears down his checks. He must have been thinking of her unfortunate fate. He must have wondered if he had anything to do with it. He must have been wondering what else he could have done to save her. He didn't share her amorousness but cared deeply about her despite knowing who she was all along. He did noticed she had changed, he did feel and believe she cared about him as in the last night with her he felt a single tear leaving her eyes in the darkness of such a cold night. Little did he know he was indeed the reason for her demise more than the SYN for simply being a real gent in a land full of theatrics.

Chatter spread throughout the SYN at sunset and all Orla could find is that Swana was passing by and saw her. Nothing more mentioned by Swana or of their chatter. Orla quickly tried to comfort Adam that it was not a hit and no one's fault. But he still believed he could have done more vying for her and that the SYN and Family are also to blame.

That night Anan was scared of punishment for losing Adam. He wasn't going to mention he did but then used Sigi's tragedy as an excuse for losing him. For Anan, it was all part of moiling and all he cared about is his own fate, coins and reputation.

THE ABODES

Orla. Good day Mr Suave.

Adam. Good day Orla.

Orla. Drowsed well?

Adam. I tried to but I couldn't.

Orla. Still thinking about her?

Adam. Please don't!... Apologies, I didn't mean this tune. You mean more to me than her and all inhabitants. I was just thinking about Os who might be going through what Sigi was going through.

Orla. Don't apologize, I admire that you care. Still, I might become angry because you are becoming a wondering awl and I have always been a joyful bird. That could be an issue.

dam. How could watching you drowse and admiring your beauty until sunrise be an issue?

Orla. You mean in the future, but my chatter is of the

present time, I meant the deputation. when I am bound to you I won't be able to drowse. I don't trust those eyes.

Adam. I should be the one scared of whatever else you could do to me. I don't want to wake up with a contraption inside my heart.

Orla. Brilliant idea so I know if it ever beats for someone else.

Adam. I can no longer tell who is more lethal you or Sigi.

Orla. Again with Sigi... Let's just chat about the deputation.

Adam. What's new?

Orla. Nothing new just old affairs I thought you would want to know about.

Adam. No new plans by SYN? that's a surprise, running out of sabotaging ideas or taking a summer break.

Orla. The deputation is on going as we suspected it. The plan is to run you dry so you lose your confidence in yourself and when the time comes you accept your fate - their plans for you - That will take time and I now understand they have unlimited fresh Os to carry on. I don't know about the Family's plans for you though.

Adam. So they want to break my pride to chose their side or lose my mind or leave and hide.

Orla. Dear inhabitants, Adam the poet.

Adam. You think I am losing it?

Orla. My dear Adam, you opened our eyes and we are the ones losing it over you.

Adam. So what's with the old affairs? Please tell me you didn't read my rolls.

Orla. I asked an O of mine learning mind analysis to read your rolls as I heard of how irrepressible you are and she might want to understand such a buoyant mind for her research. We both went through them instead and she is starting to like you too. So I thought to myself great! One more admirer.

Adam. I only care about one admirer. She is keeping me busy enough and I don't mind it.

Orla. Alright. Let me read the notes I took. Want to guess Os you came across?

Adam. Gents or damsels?

Orla. You had all kinds, a long list indeed. Want to start guessing the gents?

Adam. Rahwano

Orla. How did you know?

Adam. He was very annoying and nebby. How about Saran? He was too adhesive.

Orla. Him too. Forgetting someone?

Adam. Don't say Konsy!

Orla. Yes him. You couldn't figure him out.

Adam. I thought of it. He was generous with his coins and time. His story, dark past and lust with his multiple amours didn't fit or compliment his old dogma, attitude and respectful post.

Orla. Worry not of his coins, the SYN restitutes him. You know he almost implicated you to break the land's dictums but you refused to benefit from it. Why?

Adam. I might be short on coins but I want to live a decent life without breaking anything or anyone. I wouldn't have entertained such an idea.

Orla. You don't seem to requite their sins although you could. Another character I admire about you.

Adam. I do care but I also don't vie in dirt with a creature that enjoys it. More importantly, I believe some might leave such dirt to be cleansed someday. Who am I to deny them such a chance? A few might even go on to save a few more souls and the thought of it alone makes me smile.

Orla. I read their rolls and chatter of you. The tune changed toward the end of their deputations with you. You changed them they just won't dare to admit it.

Adam. And the damsels?

Orla. I don't want to remind you of any. Many of them were Os anyways and you treated them well, you then escaped quickly. Some weren't Os but received an unexpected visit from the SYN when you gave enough signs you liked them. They looked the other way in fear.

Adam. I noticed that too. They were frightened. I wish the best for them. It was all meant to be so one day you be with me.

Orla. I want to believe it was all destiny. The SYN made us forget in such a belief.

Adam. Believe it like I do. There is something above the SYN, above me and You.

Orla. Speaking of destiny, S34's honey was destined to be in L1 Land.

Adam. Not surprised. It gained fame in L3. I heard L1 is a colossal market. Do you know who's autarchy carried it there.

Orla. A young gent with links to S34. With a colossal backing.

Adam. I know where this is going.

Orla. Yes, the Family's backing.

Adam. At least our mountain inhabitants will rejoice, I just hope it remains pure.

Orla. The more I know you, the more I amour you. You look for the pleasantness ignoring all the bitterness.

Adam. Destiny is highly palatable if we don't dawdle on its bitterness.

Orla. Before I forget. I checked on your future Abodemate.

Adam. And?

Orla. Not an O, used to be a casual subject and is now cleared so you are geared up.

Adam. Are you saying no more Orbs?

Orla. As far as I can read nothing mentioned in any rolls.

Adam. Such a surprising breath of freedom.

Orla. I presumed they would give up eventually. Your archery was costly enough for you and a lesson for everyone.

Had these two known better, they would have feared the Abodemate more than any O. Being a former subject should've been alarming to Orla. If a seasoned O had successfully discovered the Abodemate's vulnerabilities, he could utilize them in hidden off-rolls deputations even years later so no other Os aside from him and the Abodemate could see any danger coming to Adam. The sudden absence of Orbs should've made Orla wonder nonetheless. It could be a preparation to distance the SYN from any involvement in what's to come.

Orla. Your Abodemate seems amiable, a bit chatty but amiable.

Adam. Affirmative, I bond with him.

Orla. I am just surprised Anan and Swana are still assigned to you and not complaining of any lack of excitement.

Adam. Should I be worried?

Orla. No, everything seems fine... For now at least.

It was a matter of time before Adam noticed a strange change in the behavior of his amiable Abodemate. He turned from curious and chatty to nervous and quiet. Adam had asked Orla for any change in the Abodemate's rolls or his own but the response was comforting. Soon enough the Abodemate presented a different darker side that Adam didn't expect but didn't bother him either. The Abodemate was leaving an unidentified substance in their shared entertainment zone and Adam was not keen on asking the Abodemate of his dark, possibly illegal, personal desires. Adam might wanted to give him sound advice but didn't want to create any tension. Adam finally recognized the smell of the substance, it was a prewar religious inhaler called Quro used in the mountains of S34 that gives the worshipper a supposed divine connection. Adam is now more curious if the Abodemate is using a now forbidden spiritual practice similar to one used by some in S34. He let it be for a couple of nights until a pleasant chatter unfolded between them.

Adam. I meant to ask you out of curiosity, what are these substances for?

Abodemate. Nothing Adam, will have a chatter about them someday. It's too late and I need to drowse for a while before moiling for coins.

Adam. Have an easy one then.

Abodemate. Thanks Adam.

By the next morning, Orla would learn how far the SYN's arrows have surpassed legitimate targets, far beyond any USS. Those dark venomous arrows were fast approaching and Orla needed to react fast to save Adam.

Orla. Adam wake up!!

Adam. Yes Orla... You sound edgy.

Orla. Your Abodemate is entrapping you! He reported you having illegal substances inside the abode. The Rozzers will arrive soon to confirm and he will be the hidden witness.

Adam. That recreant!.. No wonder he never wanted to chat about them. What should I do? I don't want to touch them or hide them to be more implicated.

Orla. I just left you an otic contraption by the abode's back wall. Use the memorizer inside it to capture him mentioning the substance, and pressure him to say anything valuable to discharge you of accountability.

Adam. My smart amorous Orla. I will find an excuse to wake him for moil.

Adam. Hey.. wake up. You were in serious chatter while drowsing and mentioned my name I thought you called me. You also mentioned a few matters I couldn't understand. I also remembered you telling me you needed to moil early so I made warm refreshing beverages for both of us.

Abodemate. Thanks Adam but I don't recall requesting you to wake me up. What kind of chatter?...I meant while I was drowsing.

Adam. I am always looking for what's best for you. You mentioned inhaling substances. Speaking of which, I wanted to try them if you don't mind as I never got to try them in our mountains, kind of similar. I just want to clear my pate.... I just haven't seen you use them so I wanted to ask you if you tried them. How did you acquire them?

Abodemate. I didn't but you can definitely try them if you want. '*No, they were left here by another guest*'.

Adam. Now that I am thinking about it, I don't want to try anything that you haven't brought yourself. That's all I needed you to mention my great Abodemate ... You can go back to drowsing .... for now.

Orla. Great work Adam! He confessed they weren't yours. That was close and viscous!

Adam. Thanks to you! I don't even know how to deal with him now. I need to find another abode quickly.

Orla. I will help you too. He might have noticed your reaction to the his confession.

Anan. You know what I had to do to stop the Rozzers' visit from happening?!! Your incompetence got the Syndicate officially involved in this. I shouldn't have trusted your kind. You can forget the remaining coins.

Abodemate. He came to me asking about the substances when I had barely woke up. What am I supposed to tell him they are his? He seemed to know! So I searched the abode and found an otic contraption.

Anan. Where is the memorizer?

Abodemate. There was none inside it. I am now worried about my reputation.

Anan. Your reputation means nothing. Be grateful that I haven't decided to send you back to your miserable Land.

Abodemate. My land is not miserable. Inhabitants your kind are miserable enough to see everything as such even in this beauteous Land. My Land was enchanting before the earthly war and one day it shall return.

Anan. You will have to pay for such a failure but for now, find out if Adam suspected your intentions... You might want to spread words of his delusional mind in case he starts to spread words of your intentions.

Abodemate. Adam doesn't have such a dark character.

Anan. I was nice by saying if you want. It's not up to you. Or do I need to remind you of our old little chatter?

Abodemate. Give me time and I will think of something.

Such entrapments by individual Os might never be revealed or written in any rolls. Seasoned Os such as Anan have utilized vulnerable subjects to even entrap other Os. And more frequently for their own lust and pleasure. Such hidden illegal deputations are used by sordid Os who lost any morality after seeing all that the SYN does but is hard to capture, for capturing them will devolve the ground beneath their feet halting their crawl to freedom and an opportunity to put a leash around their necks by the SYN for the rest of their lives.

Abodemate. Adam... My kinfolk will be visiting me soon and I need the abode to myself.

Adam. Delighted it came from you. Already on it, just need a bit of time.

Abodemate. They are coming soon.

Adam. As I said I am on it.

Abodemate. Please leave! You brought mental hardship to my peaceful life. Please leave!!

Adam. Fine, I will... You seem distressed. I can help if you tell me what troubles you.

Orla. Help him after what he did?

Adam. I know he didn't mean it. He is now asking me to understand and forgive without even thinking clearly.

Orla. I became aware of another matter, he began to spread words of your 'woozy mind'.

Adam. Mine? That's a first. Where?

Orla. A local hearsay gathering. He could be worried about any exposure or preparation for something worse that you might "do to yourself"

Adam. I am leaving tomorrow even if I drowse by the beachside. I feel sorry for him still.

Orla. I hear you. He must be in a disparate situation. But I care about you more as you are the victim of all of this.

Adam. Sometimes I wonder if it was my fault. If he hadn't met me he would have had a peaceful life as he said.

Orla. No Adam. He would have been used for another secretive dirty affair. His lack of courage brings him bad luck.

Adam. So I am the bad luck?

Orla. Break it Adam! You know what I mean!

Adam. I do my Amour, I now do.

This is what makes Adam rare, he does care. There are a few inhabitants the like of him. The kind that should be in charge of inhabitant's affairs for they have the kindness, intelligence, patience, forgiveness, courage and hope that are required to steer our collective ship to a safe shore. Adam might not have the experience; still, he never passes judgment without wearing everyone's raiment. This can't be the aim of the SYN, maybe the Family's using the patron. Entrapping a free soul such as Adam's will eradicate most of these admired qualities should he accept such fate. Only time and Os will tell if Adam bows to anyone but his virtuousness.

Orla. My dear Adam... I found a cordial abode.

Adam. Exciting... Where?

Orla. With an old matron. She lives on the main floor and you can live in the cordial cellar.

Adam. Less exciting. Is that what my state of affairs has come to?... If only my kinfolk find out, I will be on the first ship back.

Orla. I haven't finished! The abode is across from mine and has a back door...

Adam. Orla are you saying...

Orla. Yes! Yes!

Adam. And the old matron?

Orla. Her name is Rosa... in her later years and alone.

Her bidie-in just passed away two nights prior to this. I have been visiting their needs before then. Now it will be you assisting her and she doesn't mind me staying over. She doesn't know what I do other than being a Tutee... She won't tell anyone of you and me.

Adam. I couldn't be happier but I am uneasy about the risk you could be taking. If an O sees you coming is what I mean.

Orla. No one can... the back road has a dead end I could just hub cross to yours being masked.

Adam. And the coins?

Orla. More excitement! She will tout at the front that an old matron in need of regular assistance for a coins-free stay.

Adam. And I will be strolling randomly and see the sign right?

Orla. Our mind contraptions were meant for each others!

Adam. How amorous!

The execution of the plan began the following night. No more chances to take with the Abodemate. Adam stepped out of the abode and sauntered slow enough this time to intentionally give Anan enough chance to follow him. He wandered for vast distances around various areas seeing multiple signs of available abodes while chatting with owners asking them for time to think of the coins needed. Anan was marking all potential abodes so he can revisit them to either sabotage the deal or ask for cooperation. Adam finally arrives at the old matron's abode and sees the sign Orla has just installed. A couple of damsels were already in chatter with Rosa hoping to accept them when Adam arrived. Having been depicted by Orla, Rosa recognized Adam and apologized to the damsels professing that a gent would do more demanding moil in such a dated abode. Adam thanked the old matron for the acceptance and Anan was by the entrance hearing it all. He is now in a dilemma of how to persuade such an old matron not in need of coins to cooperate and with no apparent inhabitants she cares about that could be used to persuade her. He immediately contacted the SYN to send over her rolls. It seemed she has always been a repel with her late bidie-in having no fear or close inhabitants to care about. Anan knows it will be risky to ask her for any favors and need to find a way to ruin this deal for Adam so he continues with his struggle.

Adam moves in the same night to the new abode and had a delightful chatter with Rosa. He made her edibles using S34's old ways in her firecooker that she hadn't used for a while and kept a piece for the expected guest.

Rosa. You reminded me of my amorous bidie-in when we first met. He was the gent you are now, cherishing the old ways.

Adam. I am sure he was delighted to serve such an amorous damsel.

Rosa. I can see why she likes you.

Adam. I am not sure who you are referring to as I am bound to no one.

Rosa. Right! I forgot.

Orla has asked Rosa not to be mentioned and promised to explain the reason someday. The old matron had forgotten but smiled when Adam reminded her.

Rosa. I don't need to know everything about you Adam but it's enough to see such an alluring gent with such a radiant smile serving such old matron delicious edibles.

Adam. The pleasure is all mine. You have given me a great opportunity and a cozy abode. I will not disappoint you and will always be of service.

Rosa. The edibles you made were delicious. I suggest you keep some in your basement for when you are famine.

She said that with a smile on her face knowing who could join him at night. Rosa must have felt a sense of relief to pay back Orla for her kindness toward her and her late bidie-in.

Late that night Adam hears a gentle knock in the back door to the basement. His heart must have been racing once again. He rushed to the door knowing who was waiting. He opens and sees Orla again under the rain wearing a hooded jacket. He quickly but gently grabs her shoulders towards him giving her a hug and a decorous kiss on her forehead.

Adam. I am sorry if I kept you waiting.

Orla. I just arrived.

Adam. But you are very wit...

Orla. A short distance but too much rain that I didn't mind.

Adam. Let me take your jacket. Have a seat I'll bring you something warm.

Adam is so calm and not bantering with her as he usually does. He seems a little nervous. This is the first time they are together alone inside an abode and without any fear or care of others' affairs but theirs. He makes a speciality beverage with a splendid honey of his own in the cellar's firecooker.

Adam. Have this.. it will warm you up.

Orla. Thanks Adam, smells scrumptious.

Adam. Was it easy to find the back door? I was worried you would knock on the wrong door in such darkness and find a more suave gent.

Orla. That would be your token to bring another dazzling damsel to such a cozy cellar.

Adam. I am not looking for anyone else.

Orla. Me neither...

Adam. I am glad you are here.

Orla. Me too.. Now tell me... what do you make of such an abode?

Adam. A little dated but has a great feel to it. I can sense it was built with idolatry and honorable coins.

Orla. They are honorable inhabitants indeed. I am lucky to be their cotenant.

Adam. They are more lucky to be yours. Her words, not mine... Speaking of whom, She asked me to keep some edibles for you. Famish?

Orla. Your edibles? I won't say no to S34's edibles.

Adam. Give me a minute.

While Adam is warming up edibles in the fire cooker, Orla starts roaming around checking Adam's cellar and belongings. Smelling his perfumes and attires. Touching his hairbrush and shades. This is her first time being calm while viewing an inhabitant's belongings and not feeling guilty about it. She is at last truly invited into someone's life without any theatrics. This moment alone is enough happiness for her. A real moment that many Os long for.

After savouring the edibles, they both shared a tranquil gaze and Adam hesitantly kissed her on the lips and made an amorous advance which Orla resisted and said in a lower tune, almost a whisper 'I am not here for this Adam. I just adore the tranquillity of you holding me' She then tossed her luxuriant auburn hair on his shoulder. Adam wrapped his arm around her and gave her another decorous kiss on the forehead.

They kept gazing at each other in silence. Such a Pulchritudinous redhead with such a Suave gent. She fell asleep in his arms and he kept still until he fell asleep too until sunrise.

Orla. An amorous bright day Mr. Adam.

Adam. Oh Great, the guest woke up before me.

Orla. Who's the guest? I have known this abode before knowing you. I also made edibles like I have done here a few times before. An F3 favorite.

Adam. I am the guest indeed.

While savouring her edibles, he praised it and then went into quite deep thoughts. Orla couldn't resist asking.

Orla. I can't read your thoughts Adam. Share what you want.

Adam. Too much is being said between the pate and the heart.

Orla. You were right, you might wake up one day with a contraption in the heart... Now tell me.

Adam. Apologies for my moves last night. I didn't know what you might have longed for.

Orla. Anything with you but I am not just anyone with you. I don't know who I am with you but not like the others. Many would be your mot. I just want to be with you.. Until I know as what.

Adam. *You are my inamorata Orla. If you won't be my mot, will you be my vrou?*

With a Radiant smile she said 'YES!' then her smile washed away quickly. She remembered her hidden life with the SYN. And corrected herself ' I meant I wish to be your vrou. But that won't be fair to you.'

Adam. That's for me decide. Unless you have another reason.

Orla. You know the reason Adam. The SYN won't allow such a forbidden Amour.

Adam. We will figure out a way. We always do.

It is true the SYN will eventually know but Orla is hiding another reason. She must have wanted to inform Adam but she is afraid he might not forgive her. Especially that reason will impact Adam more than her.

The next evening Adam returned to his Abode excited to meet Orla again for a second night but he got to hear some news that he didn't expect this quickly.

Orla. Adam, I can't come tonight. You now have orbs.. Happened while you were out. Rosa was asleep.

Adam. How dare they enter when an old matron was in. Rosa might not have made it seeing them. And why the rush!?

Orla. I am sorry Adam. At least I am glad you found an abode.

Adam. That won't be it. I will take care of it.

Orla. What's in your pate?

Adam. Just watch me tomorrow.

Adam tells Rosa he wants to rearrange the abode if she wouldn't mind and renovate it from top to bottom. He began by cleaning and throwing all unwanted furniture with her guidance then started painting some areas until he reached the cellar.

Adam. Can you now tell me where the orbs would be?

Orla. No Adam don't.

Adam. I had enough of this... But worry not.

Orla. Alright.. But don't look around just listen. On top of your left shoulder is a great spot for it.

Adam started painting all the areas when he accidentally saw a strange little contraption. He wondered if he should paint over it or just ask Rosa. He called for Rosa who said she never saw such a thing before and didn't know what it was for. Adam proceeded to take them off one by one and paint over everything else just in case.

Swana. This is not good Anan. Not good at all. Why did you rush such a work?

Anan. I had no choice we can't leave him unwatched. I need to know his next moves.

Swana. The patron won't be happy about this.

Anan. I don't need a reminder, let me be.

Swana. Better me telling you no more Orbs for a while than a committee.

The SYN won't be kind to anyone who makes such mistakes. They will have to cool things off for a while before resuming with other steps. They won't make a move when Adam and the Rosa are wondering.

Orla. You did it!

Adam. I won't let anything stop me from gazing at your Elysian eyes.

Orla. I was truthfully nervous but I am glad you did.

Adam. What edibles are you craving for tonight?

Orla. Ask Rosa, and make her forget her woes. I am fine with anything.

Adam. She has been spoiled and gave me enough signs to spoil you.

Orla. Any L34s would be great.

Adam. I will take a walk in the park and think of something special before I gaze at your eyes tonight because when I do, I can't think of anything else.

Orla. Later my Amour.

Adam. Later.

Swana. May I have the pleasure of sharing the seat?

Adam. You may have all the pleasure.

Swana. How about the pleasure of being with such a lonesome handsome gent? Must be tedious fending off all the damsels in the park who crave your company.

Adam. Sounds that you say this often. And no, it's not tedious if the heart isn't looking back at them.

Orla. ADAM! THIS IS SWANA! She is the O assigned to you!

Swana. I guess you are right. They are meritorious. They are never real on the inside to look back at them, they only look at you for outer pleasure. I would too if you allow me.

Adam. Does she know?

Orla. I don't think she does ... just watch it.

Adam. Every girl has a beautiful soul in the inside, some just have dirt covering it's shine.

Swana. You mean an avalanche of dirt sweeping it away altogether.

Adam. I beg to differ, I believe their souls are temporarily too weak to shine. Although undivulged, the source of the soul can't even be dented. I believe it's as strong as a diamond. It might be covered with dirt from abuse and neglect but once Amour showers it and washes it's past away we get to see what a beauteous diamond it is and why it lasts forever. Only a wise gent can confidently appreciate the difference without an early judgment. And only a lucky gent can find, polish and keep the shining one.

Swana. My life would have been different had I met a gent like you before... Now tell me Adam. Why did you feel immense sorrow for Sigi?

Orla. That's not good Adam.

Adam. How do you know my name? A friend of Sigi?

Swana. Let's just cut to meat, shall we? Orla must have told you something about us and what we do.

Adam. I don't understand. Who is Orla?

Swana. Don't worry the Syndicate doesn't know about your Amorous tryst or I wouldn't be here alone.

Orla. She saw us. It doesn't mean she knows much.

Adam. Oh that Orla. I only went on a tryst with her once. Hard to remember all the names.

Swana. I admire that you are a protective gent but it's too late for that. You should have thought about it before your reckless tryst. Now listen attentively. I can walk away and inform the Syndicate about you too and that will be the end of it or you can answer my questions and accept my offer.

Orla. Still don't say anything.

Adam. I am listing.

Swana. I can convince the Syndicate to make you an offer with lots of coins if you join us and they will not hear of Orla's betrayal.

Adam. I appreciate the offer but I can not be useful to whatever the Syndicate is.

Swana. We will think of something. You could roam and discover all the far lands while moiling for us. We could make a gent like you our star oppo in S34 or even its Chief in time.

Adam. What's an oppo? Plus, I am not into such affairs. Nor interested in such coins.

Swana. I don't think you understand the situation that Orla is in Mr. Adam. I guess the Syndicate will have something better to offer when I am gone. Later Adam.

Adam. WAIT! You and I can make a deal that doesn't involve the Syndicate. Just keep Orla and my land out of it and keep the coins too.

Orla. Adam!

Swana. That's what I was hoping you would say since Sigi truly believed in you. You will sacrifice for Amour not coins and might. I don't need anything from you and worry not, you, as Orla, will be safe, the trulls at the Syndicate shall not know from me.

Adam. Why would you do this for us?

Swana. Tell me first. Why did you treat Sigi kindly knowing

who she was all along? And don't tell me you didn't know.

Adam. She didn't have a shining soul but a rare beauteous diamond in the inside and I was trying to wash the dirt away, I just didn't have the time to polish it. We lost such a comely soul.

Swana. You might have polished mine while watching how you cherished her and the sorrow you felt for her even after knowing her sins. I will feel better if I let you polish more diamonds as hers. More importantly, I promised her....It's not worth mentioning, but I also gave up valuable coins to leave the Syndicate this week and I don't tend to moil in the last few days. Your deputation and Sigi's tragedy had enough of me. Take care of that spoiled harlot of yours... Goodbye Adam.

Adam. Best of time being free Swana.

Orla. And just like that she is gone while I didn't even know what to say. Didn't expect and don't know what to make of this.

Adam. I think she was genuine. We have nothing but to expect anything.

Orla. I could have made up some excuse but she came to you not me. I don't know Adam. I will have a chatter with her or ask an O to look into her rolls.

Adam. No need Orla. I have met enough Os to tell when they lying, she wasn't... she is tired like Sigi was in the last few days.

Indeed Swana was candid and drained, more than she has ever been in years. Adam was right again. Swana has relinquished so many coins not waiting until her promised early retirement. She gave up all coins from Adam's deputation too but she still has a callow mind to believe the SYN will let her be in peace, *once an O, always an O*. Nonetheless, Orla and Adam were cautious for a few days not meeting or taking purposeless risk. Adam started being semi-normal again and taking his usual stroll.

THE POOR POET

Orla. I am glad you are easing your mind, I am too.

Adam. The land is shining, and the smell is ravishing. I wish I was holding your hand right now.

Orla. One day Adam, One shining day.

Adam. It's that hope that's keeping me vying.

Orla. Adam!... You see the gent across from you?

Adam. Singing?

Orla. No, the bearded blue-eyed vagrant gent. Poor poet, his beard wasn't all white the last time I saw him.

Adam. Don't say, an O?

Orla. Used to be, how did you guess?

Adam. You only mention oppos Orla. You have such a diverse life.

Orla. Mr. Adam, be grateful for such a free mentor.

Adam. You mean a tutor? I am not trained to be an O.

Orla. Right, you are beyond us all, Mr. Adam.

Adam. Feel my smile?

Orla. I do but not your heart.

Adam. It's beating even though you can't feel it.

Orla. Maybe I can... Back to the poet. Affirmative, he was an O. The patron mentioned him once and gave him coins while we were in a nearby deputation.

Adam. What happened to him?

Orla. He lost it. The Patron said the SYN wronged him after all the years he moiled for them. He was in a forbidden Amour. An Amour he lost but couldn't prove the SYN's doing. He now says vocables that rhyme but don't make sense, inhabitants still call him the poor poet though, out of sympathy I presume.

Adam. I will give him some coins for his lost Amour maybe hear a beauteous poem.

The poet looked at Adam's coins in the piece of cloth in front of him as if they were a treasure, he then dazed at Adam in wonder.

Adam. I wish I had more, you seem like a kind gent.

Poet. Spending Coins won't help you understand why you and me in such a poppets' land.

Adam. I didn't know I needed to understand anything.

Poet. You don't for being a far-to-reach star. The Puppets' Land outsource a burning star, a star that just wants to belong. The star's smile shines sorrow from afar under our skin the feeling would be wrong. It will give us warmth, a lesson, and a scar so we remember to be strong. Different schools for the same bazaar. No magic, just a puppets' land all along.

Adam. One day I'll understand kind gent. I will see you again.

Poet. *'I will be seen by a soul that can see. The pure soul in you not in me'.*

It's evident that the Patron's chatter with Orla has been in preparation for something beyond the SYN's aim. He trusted her with hidden roles and old souls of the SYN that few know about, the like of the poet's. Adam now walking in silence and no one knows his thoughts not even Orla. But the poet seems to have touched Adam's soul and ignited a flame within him that he can't seem to understand or extinguish.

Orla. I told you he lost it, the poor poet.

Adam. I don't think he did, we did.

Orla. What do you mean?

Adam. I felt his pain and wisdom Orla. I believe he didn't lose anything just not interested in it all. But he seems to chat with me in a way that I feel but Can't fully understand.

Orla. Adam, it's too warm outside, you need a beverage.

Adam. I am serious Orla.

Orla. Just confirming.

Two days and nights have passed and Adam is still thinking of the Poor Poet and decides to revisit him. The poor poet was lying down in a road corner not far from Adam's Abode and writing in a scrap of paper. Adam now recognizes him and is eager to stop by for another mysterious wisdom. He came prepared with more coins this time for the poet.

Poet. I told you coins are for the poppets of the land, must be hard for you to understand.

Adam. How did you know it's me?

Poet. Your soul.. The ilk is hard for puppeteers to control.

A group of inhabitants pass by Adam and the poet. Mocking the two. 'I guess the crazy one found his saviour' 'Young gent don't waste your coins on him'. Adam responded 'Helping inhabitants in need is never a waste, everything else is'. one gent in the well-dressed group responded 'This gent is the waste' Adam looked at him and replied 'He must have had a more honorable life than being a dolt like you. Maybe one day you become him but I doubt you will ever be this wise or kind.' Orla interrupted 'Don't engage, they sound like provocateurs the SYN would send to test or entrap you'. Another gent responded. 'why don't you join him then and shovel his never-ending pill of shredded paper, actually don't, this land wastes enough coins to this loser, and we don't want more'. A third continued by saying 'Don't give hope to a lost gent to be a poet at such an age. He writes and writes and it goes to waste eventually instead of moiling' Adam looks at them with disgust' There are those who save your kind in silence, I wish they were the ones making the noise and you're the ones silent. Move on!...' The group saw a seriousness in Adam's eyes, enough to know something about him so they walked away with a smirk on their faces.

Adam. I am sorry you had to deal with such inhabitants.

Poet. Pity me not but those gone astray, for the jingle of coins cover their dogma's say, pity poppets fearing their way and liveries taking their pay.

Adam. I will remember this kind gent. Take care.

Orla. Poor poet. He went through so much and still does. Still admiring his poems?

Adam. I believe I understand them.

Orla. What does he mean by all that?

Adam. The Family

Orla. What does he have to do with the Family?

Adam. Anything else the patron mentioned to you of him?

Orla. Nothing that I could remember but his lost Amour and then losing it. I was curious to look into his rolls but there were none.

Adam. Why would you want to look into his rolls?

Orla. I thought I would find rolls of great romance and tragedy. Now tell me?

Adam. I believe he meant the Family will turn every land into a puppets' land.

Orla. Just like the Laman Hamlet!

Adam. Just like the Laman Hamlet.

The poet is indeed mentioning the Family. But also The *'Subterranean Oligarchs'*. It's palpable that Adam is beginning to better understand post-SFV affairs, even more than trained oppos, the likes of Orla with access to valuable rolls. He seems to fathom the far-reaching influence of the Family, the seduction of inhabitants, the role the SYN plays in it all. Still; he has little to no knowledge of the scattered power of the Subterranean Oligarchs as few ever clearly understand such collective-scattered might. The Family has a great influence over most lands and coins to helm it; however, the Subterraneans are collectively collaborating to enforce more power for the benefit of their elite, not their inhabitants or the Family's. The implementation of their might is through enough deluded innocent inhabitants who are blindly moiling to maintain such power. Subterraneans had enough coins to build lavish underground zones to protect their affluent members before the SFV which, some whisper, caused it with the Family, leaving their less fortunate inhabitants to perish believing in old dogmas. Soon enough after the SFV, Subterraneans along with the Family began searching for fertile surviving and far lands such as F3. Subterraneans have less coins thus they embezzle the Family periodically and direct oppos' fury towards them without mentioning their aim and their alliances. All this while retaining their innocence. Subterraneans have also vetoed old dogmas of all lands but impalpably kept theirs to dominate their new deluded inhabitants. The Family is aware but collaborates with them nevertheless since they don't have enough inhabitants to rebel. The same reason they rely on SYN's oppos beside theirs.

None of them; however, can wash their hands from intruding into surviving and far lands.

Unlike the Subterraneans', The Family's influence is very concentrated, thus adroitly influencing the selection of chosen servants. Chosen servants, whether aware or not, act as legitimizers to the Family's plans being chosen by unaware inhabitants who then lose the capacity to complain. Chosen servants pen dictums and USS, then name judges who follow such dictums which ultimately protect the Family and the SYN. A truly vicious cycle that inhabitants and even some decent Chief Chosen Servants(CCS)such as the current one in F3 keep running through totally oblivious that until his opponent, who was groomed by the Family, takes over.

The poor poet would have longed to edify this to Adam and all inhabitants if he could. He is of a subterranean bloodline and had the opportunity to truly discover his old dogma in searching for meaning after his lost forbidden Amour. The Family's oppos wanted him gone for he was fearless with them before and after his amorous pain and then becoming godly but the Subterraneans intervened after he lost it. He was not a fan of either but was hurt by his bloodline and their new way of going astray.

The SYN has been instrumental in shaping all of this and all that has emerged since the SFV. The SYN is like the glue that bonds all the pieces together. But what happens when you put too much glue in anything? That's what the Family advocated for.

THE UPRISING

A few more days passed and Adam was trying to communicate with Orla to see if he could finally meet her again but she wasn't communicating. He got worried; yet, there was nothing he could do but to wonder around the market. He couldn't see the poor poet at his usual resting corner. He continued and saw a few of his popular shops closed without an explanation. Sigi crossed his mind so he tried to pass by the Riddle Bridge but it was closed by the Rozzers apparently a few mysterious incidents happened overnight.

Orla. Hi Adam.

Adam. Where have you been all day? I was worried!

Orla. Apologies... I know you tried to communicate.

Adam. Everything Fine?

Orla. No one knows Adam ... No one!

Adam. What do you mean? what happened?

Orla. HAPPENING!! An uprising, a revolt maybe a REVOLUTION!!

Adam. Where?

Orla. Within the SYN's invisible walls and beyond them. All Os are on edge thanks to you and whoever ignited it!

Adam. ME!? I was at my abode... peacefully.

Orla. Your resilience and peaceful life caused this. You taught Os there is a joyful honourable life to be lived without the darkness of the SYN, our sin, as a requisite.

Adam. Orla,... Please Come, let's have a chatter.

Orla. I can't. Everyone is Goosey!. They are looking for whoever caused it.

Adam. me?

Orla. NO! An O leaked all your rolls even sensitive ones to all Os, supreme inhabitants and even the CCS!

Adam. The Chief Chosen Servant? He knows of me?

Orla. Yes! Your rolls were leaked in a way that showed your innocence and good character. The Family's role, Sigi's Amour for you and her demise. Os are now reputing all concurrent deputations demanding answers for them. Your deputation exposed their rotten ways and the duplicity within.

Adam. When can I see you?

Orla. I don't know Adam. For the first time, I am not sure. I am shivering although I am wearing my wool coat. Nothing like this has ever emerged before my eyes, I feel hope mixed with fear and an inevitable reform, thanks to you!

Adam. So Os no longer want to obey knowing the SYN has gone astray... Tell me the family is losing a grip of their whip!?

Orla. Nothing clear Adam but we are all cautiously optimistic.

Adam. Will you be safe? free? Come run away with me!

Orla. My absence will raise suspicion. Worry not, most of us will be safe. We contain things within.. It seems enough word spread beyond the SYN though… Let's hope our CCS courageously intervenes.

Adam. I believe he is a decent gent.. How much courage he has left to cleanse such venom for F3's sake is yet to be seen. Inhabitants deserve his courage nonetheless, especially with the chance his shady opponent might take it over.

Hello Orla.

Orla. What... Who is this?!

Papino. You can call me Papino but I am not important, you and Adam are. I can hear the fright in your inner voice. You must have a heap of questions but fear not, I shall ease some of your perturbations. I am just not sure of the number of days we have.

Adam. What is happening Orla?

Papino. Of course. How could I forget Mr. Adam is connected.

Orla. How did you…

Papino. The contraption? Oh well, we might have a couple of days at least so let's have a chatter.

Adam. Orla! Who is this? why can I hear him?!

Papino. She doesn't know Adam but I will explain. I was assigned by the SYN to watch the Patron and you Adam and anyone involved in your deputation. Didn't expect the little experiment your father allowed you to conduct Orla. Lucky for you two the SYN doesn't know.

Adam. Her father? Orla?... Are you going to say something?

Orla. I will Adam I promise I will... How did you connect to this Papino?

Papino. You should have known the SYN never trusts anyone including the one who quelled my tenure and coerced the damsel I adored. *Your father, the patron.* Luckily for you too, No one else has a contraption thanks to your single prototype. I then picked up the signal from you after Adam's surgery. I can hear and feel it all ... If only such a contraption existed before the SFV.

Orla. You gassed my abode! The reason I overslept that day... why are you telling us all of this?

Papino. Your father is taken, I presume they didn't enjoy your Amorous Tryst or the uprising. Whatever the reason it's irrelevant at the present time. But it's a matter of time before they come for us all... I am tired of it all, you two; however, should leave to live it all. And I want to be of assistance.

Orla. Why would you help us?

Papino. We all are asking why when someone offering help. The state we are in thanks to the SYN...I adored your mother but that's not it. You and Adam changed me.

Orla. You knew my momma?

Papino. She was my Amour. I trust your father never mentioned her past. I left her after the SYN gave me an ultimatum... She either joins us or I leave her without an elucidation after I committed the Sin of falling for her, an outsider. I wasn't as courageous as you with Adam. I left her to live her life away from my sin with the SYN. Away from our lies and deception. I cared about her dearly, but I wasn't brave enough to tell her the truth about who I am, let alone ask her to run away with me. Soon enough The SYN sent the Patron to seduce her, she accepted him after losing me and then her post, she was vulnerable. It was all in their plan and that broke my heart. Watching you and Adam made me realize I wasn't caring, I was just a coward for leaving her... Don't be like me, don't make my mistake, you two need to endure for your amour and need not be sure, for losing amour has no cure. Just run away while they are absorbed in the uprising.

Orla. It takes courage and immense Amour to leave someone you adore Papino... Did you start the uprising?

Papino. Another oppo started the uprising and I let it happen.

Orla. Who?

Papino. Anan. He is a mole. I was watching him carefully but didn't expect him to betray the SYN. Whoever he moils for is less imperative to what he did, what was needed to be done a long time ago for our sake and the land, so I let him do it. Let's Keep it that way for the legitimacy of the uprising and momentum.

Adam. You two are chatting of a revolution that requires honest oppos and servants, sadly this land seems to have none. All Os seem to lie to even the dearest to them. You all will always have a sin or an embarrassing affair as a deterrence to justice so the land will have no honest Os to fall back on. I thought Orla was that one O but even she lied to me about her poppa, the patron, the gent responsible for making my life difficult... I thought you were always honest Orla. I truly trusted you.

Papino. She was mostly honest with you Adam, she isn't like him. You should trust her. Besides, she is the only one you can now trust to save you as she has always done. Prepare to leave with her soon. Orla, you need to always be honest with him he deserves it no matter how hard the truth is.

Adam. Easy for you to say Papino since you are all the same. I am not sure I can trust you again Orla. If you have any dignity left don't follow me until I remove the contraption.

Orla. Adam, you are my only Amour and kinfolk. I just didn't know when or how to tell you without the stigma. Just Wait, I will explain what went through my pate, I made an unforgivable mistake and I understand you might never forgive me... Papino, you know what they will do to you and then us after they find the contraption inside you.

Papino. Fear not darling for there will be nothing left of me and anyone entering my abode.

Orla. Don't do this... I can remove it, let us meet.

Papino. I would have been delighted to meet you both again but I am not certain we have such precious days ahead. I am certain it's time to take some of them down with me after I take care of one last thing. Just live your lives away from the SYN, I left you a gift in your mom's favourite cellar so you can live far away comfortably. Adam, you are different always remember that *'I will be seen by a soul that can see. The pure soul in you not in me.'*

Adam. THE POET!!

Orla. The Poet?

Papino. It was a pleasure meeting you Adam. Take care of her, she truly Amours you. Oh Great, hold it.. I wasn't expecting another signal this soon.... ADAM! ORLA! BE GONE NOW!!

Orla. Adam, my Amour I am coming to you, we need to leave.

Papino. Great.. I guess I won't be editing this... Hola poet speaking?

THE SYN. You will pay for betraying us Papino

Papino. Pay? How shall I, being a poor poet?

THE SYN. You ruined your legacy and your only chance at redemption. You know what will happen and no one will ever hear of you.

Papino. **I wouldn't be so sure of that...**

Printed in Great Britain
by Amazon

46108587R00088